ADVANCE

"*Brooks* is an unexpected and delightful novel that grabs you by the hand from page one, and leads you to familiar places—without ever letting you go until you read that final word. Even though this lovely Christian novel is a sweet story, gently told, it gripped me! I was riveted. The wee hours of the morning found me breathless to find out how everything could possibly turn out well for the heroine. The cast of characters were so well-drawn that they felt like real people I could meet at the store or who I'd somehow met at church sometime in the past. Kudos to DeeBee Daws for creating a gorgeous piece of literature that will appeal to readers with its wisdom and magic, as well as its carefully created and intense plotline. Five enthusiastic stars. Highly recommend!"

— Jennifer Griffith, *USA Today* bestselling, twice Swoony Award-winning author of over fifty novels, both traditionally and independently published

"We've all said, 'If these walls could talk.'

Well, DeeBee Daws' *Brooks* does just that.

A delightful story about a house with feelings, observes those who enter, and reacts to their emotions and personalities. An endearing underlying love story, with connections beyond the grave. *Brooks* will keep you guessing with twists when you least expect it."

— Debbie Ihler Rasmussen
Author, Content Editor, Ghostwriter

"Welcome to *Brooks*, come on in. Get cozy and let Dora and Len encircle you in the many layers of the journey of Brooks. Many monumental events await you. This book is a refreshing read, so get cozy and enjoy. Love the story."

– J. Jensen

"I loved this book. The story of Dora and Len was interesting and I cried a couple of times with their life events. The house named *Brooks* was almost like hearing from a real person with changes and events. I enjoyed reading it so much."

– C Sorensen

BROOKS

BROOKS

DeeBee Daws

WELDERLY PUBLISHING

Brooks
Copyright © 2024 by DeeBee Daws

All rights reserved, including the right to reproduce
distribute, or transmit in any form or by any means.

Except as permitted under the U.S. Copyright Act of 1976, no part of this book may be reproduced, distributed, or transmitted in any form or by any means, or stored in a database or retrieval system without the written permission of the authors, except in the case of brief passages embodied in critical reviews and articles where the title, author and ISBN accompany such review or article.

For information contact:
deebeedaws@outlook.com

Published by:
Welderly Publishing

Cover design by Beyond Imagination
Interior book design by Francine Platt, Eden Graphics, Inc.

This book is a work of fiction. Names, characters, places, and incidents are the product of the author's imagination or are used fictitiously. Any resemblance to actual events, locales, or persons, living or dead, is coincidental.

Paperback ISBN 978-1-958626-87-0
Ebook ISBN 978-1-958626-88-7
Audio book ISBN 978-1-958626-90-0

Library of Congress Number: 2024905465

Manufactured in the United States of America

First Edition

*Dedicated to my husband Lowell —
my biggest cheerleader, who always encourages me
to follow my heart; and to my daughter Robyn,
and my daughter-in-law Roseann.*

*"Honesty and integrity are the foundations
of good character. Always strive to do the
right thing, even when it's difficult."*

Brooks is approachable, and his warmth envelopes visitors like the comforting presence of a beloved elder. His words of wisdom are plastered on his walls and seep from his floorboards.

Brooks is not a venerable grandfather. He is not a man at all. He is a humble abode—a living testament to the enduring bond between humanity and home, and we all know there is no place like home—but this home is extraordinary, and there is no place like Brooks.

He's been around long enough to experience a variety of life within his walls and on the grounds where he proudly sits. His foundation is surrounded with greenery and roots, offering an intricate exchange system with trees, shrubs, and extraordinaire plant life. Brooks' water system bubbles with gossip, hurriedly entering his framework of lumber.

He's been devoid of human life too long and is now in for a change as he plays host to a glorious salad-like mixture of humanity.

Born in 1910, Brooks is the product of love between two people, building him of materials common to his breed and arranging those materials to reflect his destiny. The plan for him was first formulated in the minds of his builders. It was sown in the womb of nature, where his gestation proceeded. He was an extension of them, and they took great pride in their creation.

His old family name exudes strength, endurance, and emulation. They spoke his name with tenderness and often proclaimed their love for him and each other.

Once construction was complete, Brooks lifted his eaves with a smile. The studs in the walls stretched, making him taller and more robust. His furnace system hummed a little faster as he proudly began to understand his role. The sun beamed through the windows of his soul, and the front door beckoned visitors to enjoy his innermost sanctum.

Brooks was ready to protect, defend, and provide.

As time went on, the new home developed a personality. His soul took a foothold in his foundation as he matured and reflected a disposition of independence borne from the actions exhibited by his inhabitants. The house liked his name. It fit, and when he heard his creators say his name, pleasure filled him, from the attic ceiling to the basement floors. Brooks listened for ways he could add to the joy of his creators.

He comforted babies who cried, laughed with little children, and watched over his ever-present creators who cared for him. Brooks was vigilant in his mission. He never slept. The experiences of the family seeped into his walls. He lived vicariously through their sicknesses, with aches in his joists and sometimes fever-like heat beating on his roof, trickling down through his paint and soaking into his floor coverings.

When the youngsters grew up, they often disappeared only to return on odd occasions. The couple stayed on despite not being as agile as they once had been, and they continued to tend to Brooks. The house did the only thing he could do in reciprocation. He blessed them with an orchard of fruit trees, a bountiful vegetable garden, beautiful flowers, streams, and a forest of trees.

Brooks became well acquainted with joy, laughter, and love. He saw that people were different when they were "in love." They were happy and at peace with everything around them. Sometimes, they fell out of love, which was confusing to him. He tried to get counsel from those within his boundary, but they needed more information. He decided that love didn't always make sense. Brooks determined he would find contentment in his existence and look for good around him every day. This decision caused his pipes to quietly gurgle.

He felt the tenderness of mourning when the souls of his creators succumbed to physical death. He assimilated those souls into the most personal spaces of his walls. He realized that he needn't feel sad because they still existed in a contrasting yet intrinsic form.

Through the years, there had been other creator-like creatures, and Brooks' understanding of humanity increased. He was good at his job as a shelter and a perfect guardian of secrets.

This morning, from his roost on the hill, he breathed in air from his meadow. The clearness of it told him that changes were coming, and he needed to be ready to welcome them properly.

Brooks was open to change. Experience taught him to embrace it and to look for the growth it would inevitably bring.

The bright, happy light in the east was almost above the horizon, and it wouldn't take long for the dewy dampness on the leaves and grasses to dissipate. The forest was coming alive with activity as animals began another day of exploration. The watering holes were being visited, and tree branches offered places for perch. They all had ears and were not averse to spreading the gossip they saw in their habitats. Having new creators brought a sense of excitement. He was ready and the inhabitants of his expansive, forest-like grounds were organized, Everything was in place.

Soon, a dose of new life would be administered, and Brooks' existence would take on a new and different perspective.

Change is like the seasons – It keeps things fresh.

"Dora, honey, I'm leaving. I've got an inspector and an appraiser coming today. Roger's coming too, so we'll be busy the rest of the day. Are you coming out at all?"

Elbow-deep in dishwater, Dora glanced at her husband as he came in from the garage.

"No, Len. I have a mountain of laundry to get done. Don't forget we have a video call with Robyn tonight at seven. They're eighteen hours ahead of us. It's Rachel's seventh birthday, and little Lenny will want to say hi to Grumpy."

The Grant grandchildren referred to Dora and Len as Grammy and Grampy, but little Lenny's words came out as Grammy and Grumpy. Len always laughed good-naturedly, and the little man was none the wiser.

"I'm looking forward to it. I want to hear about their quarters in Australia, find out if they've seen any kangaroos," said Len.

Dora rinsed out the sink and wiped off the counters with her dishcloth. "Len, would you measure the entry and snap a picture? I want to get a mat of some kind to put there. We need one to catch dirt when people come in. I found something I like so I want to make a good match."

Len stepped back into the kitchen and wrapped his arm around her waist. He turned his wife of forty-five years to face him.

His six-foot frame towered over hers. He looked at her intently and lifted her chin.

Dora gazed into familiar blue eyes and smiled back at his handsome face. He had a full head of salt and pepper hair, and his upper lip sported a mustache. She combed through his wavy strands with her fingers. It tousled loosely about his ears and fell back into the same tufts she had tried to smooth out.

He pulled the ball cap from his back pocket and put it on.

"There," he put both arms around her. "Solves that problem. I love you." He punctuated the declaration with a gentle tug and pulled her closer.

"I'm happy, Dora. This whole experience has me looking forward to sharing more great times with you. I'm feeling alive and ready for a new adventure. I feel like I'm forty years younger. Are you happy, Dora? I want you to be."

Their eyes met swimming with memories of nearly five decades of "mostly wedded bliss." Dora buried her head in Len's chest muscles, reveling in the safety of his arms.

"I love you too, Len. Thanks for working so hard on Brooks. I'm learning to adore that old house. I'm looking forward to meeting new people and amazing experiences." She softly thumped his chest. "However, pace yourself. Between the house and your job, I worry about you. You're no spring chicken."

"Oh yeah? I'll have you know I'm a banty rooster, and when I need my hen…"

A wink and diabolical grin flashed across his face.

Dora abruptly stood on her tiptoes and kissed his lips. She still marveled at the tingle she felt at the tenderness of old love.

His mustache tickled her nose, and Len laughed at the familiar response.

"We've still got it, Dora. You're still my girl, my best girl."

Dora nodded. "And you're my guy, my best guy."

He smiled and released her. "See ya later, alligator."

"After while crocodile."

"Too soon, baboon."

Dora pushed away, grabbed his oversized lunch bag, and thrust it into his chest. She took the crook of his arm and escorted the big kid to the garage door. She laughed. "How soon, raccoon?"

She closed the door and heard Len chuckle.

He unlocked the driver's side door of his F150 Ford pickup and climbed behind the wheel.

Len's mind raced the entire fifteen-minute drive. He stopped in front of the house and was enveloped in an invisible warm welcome from a treasured old friend.

Tim and Beth Grant, Len's grandparents, built the house and then did some major construction in their later years. It was the biggest and nicest home in the county. Pete and Emma Grant, Len's parents, were the second owners. His mother was a fuss budget. She decorated the home with beautiful furnishings and made sure everything was well cared for.

They wrote a letter of their desire to leave the house to Len. However, there was not a will, so it had been stuck in probate court for nearly five years, neglected until Len and Dora took ownership. They were the third generation of Grants to own the property.

Len worked tirelessly to create Brooks Bed & Breakfast. The county had even assigned the old house a modern address, replacing the original rural free delivery one. These days, it was the Brooks house on Grouse Road, with house number two hundred and thirty-nine.

Today, his first order of business was to inspect the attic area.

He parked in the circular driveway, opened the massive front door, and carried his toolbox into the house. He turned right at the top of the stairs and headed down the hall.

Brooks was ready for another day with his new owner.

Len's feet were familiar to the grand staircase. The rope that dangled from the ceiling, anticipated his grasp. It enlivened to Len's touch when he reached for it, and obligingly, the attic door opened, and stairs disengaged.

Len climbed the steps, cleared the opening, and peered into the darkness. Light poured from the dormer window at the far end, and dust bunnies danced in the shaft from the sun. Len focused on the shapes they made. He fumbled to find a light switch at the upper right-hand corner of the wall.

Len's father had installed a bank of neon lights along the side wall when Len was a boy. They lit up with a flip of the switch, chased away the dust bunnies, and cleared the murky shapes. Neatly stacked and labeled cardboard boxes lined one wall.

Today, Len was focused on locating items to fill empty spaces throughout the house. He inspected some promising pieces of furniture and took inventory of stacked framed artwork. Next to the art, a couple of rolled-up rugs and a wooden trunk.

He stood motionless for a minute, staring at the trunk. Strangely, it seemed to beckon him. He half expected to see someone, or something step out of the shadows, and he shivered at the recollection of stories that the house was haunted. He shrugged and chided himself for such foolishness.

Satisfied he was alone, he focused on the trunk and pulled it away from the wall. It wasn't heavy, so he picked it up by the rope handles and carried it to a table.

He traced the carved filigree pattern on the lid with his fingers, and slowly opened the cover to reveal its shadowed contents. He found the flashlight on his phone but was frustrated with the lackluster beam it produced.

The first thing he saw was a colorful piece of fabric he recognized as a quilt top. Len didn't know much about handicrafts, but he easily recalled his mom and her friends gathered around quilting frames and sewing all afternoon.

Len and his friends often played under the quilts with toy cars or created artwork in their coloring books. The women interspersed their creativity with stories, laughter and exchanged advice about child-rearing. He wondered if Dora might like to finish the quilt and use it at Brooks.

Beneath the quilt top were pamphlets and rolled-up blueprints secured with string. He lifted the prints from the box, removed the binding, and unrolled the pages. He couldn't see details, but the smudges on the pages and dirty curled edges testified to the labor involved in a build. He rerolled the blueprints, lightly smacked the roll into the palm of his hand, and returned them to the trunk.

Len's eyes settled on a smaller box made of fine wood with rounded corners and the same filigree pattern carved on its lid. He retrieved the house key from his pocket. He held the key next to the pattern on the smaller box, and then the lid on the big box, recognizing the duplication of the filigree.

Once again, Len felt an invisible beckoning, or was it insight? Leather hinges held the lid of the smaller box, and he lifted it. He strained to view the contents using his phone's meager light. He lifted a tintype picture of a couple wearing dress clothes standing in front of a house. Len looked closer and realized it was this house, the one called Brooks.

He imagined these to be his grandparents and remembered their names as Beth and Timothy Grant. There were also a few trinkets in the trunk, the kind kept for sentimental value. The most notable was a polished heart-shaped stone in an unusual wire setting hanging on a silver chain. Upon closer inspection, he could see the initials BG, etched on the stone.

"Interesting," he mumbled.

At the bottom of the box was a legal-sized manila envelope with *bonds* carefully printed in bold block letters. He picked it up and heard the doorbell ring.

The front door opened. "Hello, anybody home? It's Russ. I'm here to do the inspection."

Len turned in the direction of the voice. "I'm upstairs, be there in a minute."

He put the box back where he found it and returned the rolled-up rug. Curious about the envelope's contents, he felt compelled, no it seemed to beg. Len grabbed it and hurried down the attic stairs, secured them back in place, and rushed down the hall, where he slowed his pace and started down the grand staircase.

Russ peeked around the barely opened door.

"Hi, Russ," said Len.

"Good morning, Len. I hope it's okay that I'm a few minutes early. I didn't mean to startle you."

Len pulled him across the threshold with a firm handshake.

"It's good to see you again, Russ. I'll bet you'll be as glad as I will to have this thing wrapped up."

"I don't mind, it's my job, and I especially enjoy wandering through old houses like this one. Anyway, today's visit won't take long. I need to verify some things before I write my final report."

The inspector's crew-cut hair, plaid short-sleeved shirt, khaki pants, and penny loafers echoed he was stuck in the sixties. He peered over horn-rimmed glasses perched on the tip of his nose and reached for the pencil tucked behind his ear. In his arms, he clutched a clipboard, the spring clip straining from the stack of paper.

"Glad to hear it. Feel free to roam and do what you do, I'll be in the library. Call out if you need me."

"I'll do that."

The inspector headed toward the grand staircase, and Len carried the envelope to the library and closed the door behind him. He loved the seclusion of the library and the wisdom it exuded. The walls of books, the chairs, and the sofa were all unspoken invitations to relax with a good book.

Len sat in the oversized leather office chair and pulled it closer to the mahogany desk. The chair squeaked a little as he settled into it and again when his weight shifted. He placed the envelope squarely on the desk and pulled out the contents. Inside were some kind of certificates bound with an elastic band that was so brittle it broke when Len pulled the top paper away.

He could barely read the small print. Each of the more than a dozen papers were labeled *Bearer Bonds.* Len gasped. He had never spent much time studying the stock market, but he knew a little about bearer bonds and sensed their potential. He snapped a picture of the top bond with his phone and placed everything back in the envelope minus an elastic band and closed the clasp.

He leaned back in the chair and weighed his options. He reasoned that the bonds likely belonged to his grandfather but had lay dormant in the trunk for almost three generations. Len decided he needed to talk to somebody he could trust.

He called James Brennen at the Mondale Bank and requested an attorney referral. Without reservation, Mr. Brennen suggested Jake Karvelas and gave Len the phone number. He said that Karvelas had handled several things for him as well as for the bank.

"Thanks for the referral, James. I'm coming to town this afternoon." Len wanted to secure the bonds in something better than a wooden trunk in a dusty old attic behind a century-old rug. "I hope there are some larger safety deposit boxes available."

"I'm not sure what there is but come to the new accounts desk. My girl there will help you."

"Thanks again, James. I'll be in later."

He called the attorney's office, and the woman on the other end of the phone finally relented to Len's insistence on having an appointment sooner rather than later. She agreed to a time with Mr. Karvelas the day after tomorrow. Feeling a new burst of energy, Len left the library.

Another car pulled up when he opened the front door. It was Sam, the appraiser and Len waited for him to park.

Sam was tall, lean, well-dressed, and carried a leather pouch. He had been to the house more than once and was also a family friend from the local community of Mondale.

"Good morning, Len. I'm here to finish up the appraisal, it shouldn't take long."

"Do you need me here? I have an errand to run that I need to do as soon as possible."

"As long as you don't mind my being here without you, I'm fine."

"You'll not exactly be by yourself. Russ is upstairs finishing up the inspection. He said he didn't need much time either."

"Great, Russ and I are old friends. I have your cell phone number, if I have any questions."

"Absolutely. Technology is a great thing. I'm from the old school of a dial-up phone hanging on the kitchen wall with a big, long, curly cord attached. I wasn't so sure of cell phones at first, but I'm hardly able to live without mine now."

"I know what you mean, I'm the same way. It's nice to call my teenagers when they're late coming home. Unless, they forget to charge the darn thing, at least that's the excuse they use."

The two men shook hands, and Sam said, "We'll contact you as soon as my appraisal has been filed."

Happiness ain't in fancy things, it's in the simple moments.

Mondale Bank has been operating for over forty years, and Len and Dora were among its first customers. The Grant family consisted of the two of them and a toddler back then. Their picture hung in the gallery of photos displayed on the exposed brick wall dedicated to the bank's history. Len remembered opening savings and checking accounts that day. He and Dora had joked about being "real grownups" while they stood in line. The couple even got a safety deposit box for all their most important papers. At first, the contents were scarce, but as time passed, the volume increased. Now, Len needed an even larger box to accommodate the probate papers and the bonds he found. He reassuringly touched the envelope on the truck seat as he briefly steered with one hand.

Thankfully, the bank's parking lot had few cars, so he assumed there wouldn't be much wait time. Len wanted this to be a quick trip. As he made his way to the bank door, he took out the small flat key in a secreted fold of his wallet and went directly to the "new accounts" desk. As he approached, the clerk looked up, revealing the face of an old family friend.

"Good morning, Mr. Grant, it's good to see you. What can I do for you today?"

It was Myla Dawson, an old friend of Len's younger daughter, Robyn.

"Myla, I didn't know you worked here. How nice to see your beautiful smile."

"Yeah, I've been here almost a year now. How's Robyn? I haven't heard from her in a while?"

"Oh, she's fine. Brian's been assigned to a post in Australia. Did you know that?"

"Yes, she sent me a note telling me they were packing up and moving to the land down under. She sounded excited about his new assignment. She even sent me a picture of the kids."

Len nodded. The smile on his face reflected his adoration for his baby girl. "Man, those little kids are growing up fast. I'm sure it'll be an adventure for the whole family. Please don't give up on her, Myla. She'll probably contact you as soon as she gets herself organized again. They're calling us tonight. I'll let her know I saw you today."

"Oh, that would be great, and believe me, I understand. I'll send her a quick message this evening, reminding her I'm still here leading my uneventful life. What can I do for you, Mr. Grant?"

"I have a safety deposit box here."

"Oh sure, sign this access sheet noting your box number, and I'll get you into the safe."

Myla handed Len the clipboard, took a ring of keys from a locked desk drawer, and pushed her chair away.

"Hey, hold up, Myla. There's something else."

"Oh, I'm sorry, Mr. Grant. I'm getting ahead of myself. What is it?"

"I'd like to get a larger box than the one I'm currently assigned to. I have some documents I want to add, and the box is just too small for everything."

Myla stopped and looked at Len Grant with an incredulous stare.

"This is so ironic. Until an hour ago we didn't have any large boxes available. But then, Mrs. Jensen, do you remember the Jensen's? They have seven daughters, all of them blond and pretty. Anyway, they've all grown up and moved away. Well, it seems that …"

"Myla, I'm kind of in a hurry."

"Oh, sure, but you see, the Jensen's closed their box, which means we have one large safety deposit box, and here you are. Life is so amazing sometimes."

She retrieved a looseleaf binder from her desk and turned to a labeled section in the back. She quickly found the section in question and scanned it with her pointer finger, stopping and punching the box number with an imaginary punctuation mark.

"Yes, box two thirty-nine is available. It'll only take a few minutes for me to make that transfer. I can get you water or a soda while you wait. We might even have coffee if you prefer."

"Did you say box two thirty-nine?"

Myla checked again. "Yes, two thirty-nine."

"Humph, that's interesting. Uh, no, I don't want anything, but thanks."

"I heard about you and Mrs. Grant renovating Brooks. I'm so excited for you. I want to see it when you open for business. I remember many times when Robyn and I would roam around the gardens of that old place."

In a whispered tone, she continued, "We liked to pretend it was enchanted with fairies. I love that old house. Robyn and I …"

"Myla, could we get the transfer done? I have so many things to get done today. We'll invite you out to Brooks for a pre-opening party, and we'll have a good visit. Dora would love to hear about your and Robyn's adventures at Brooks."

"Oh, sure, Mr. Grant. Sorry, as usual, I got distracted."

It only took a few minutes to complete the paperwork and get it signed before Myla handed Len a small white envelope containing the key.

"We'll need Mrs. Grant to sign the new card, so have her stop in the next time she's in town," instructed Myla as she led the way into the vault. "I'll leave you to transfer everything. Let me know when you're ready to lock up."

"You got it, and I'll tell Dora tonight about the signature card."

Len transferred the documents, including the bonds, to the larger box. He returned the container to the vault, locked it, and pocketed the envelope containing the key. He stopped at Myla's desk and said, "Thanks, Myla, I appreciate you. Have a good day." He patted her desk and strode away.

"Bye, Mr. Grant, give your wife my best."

Len waved as he walked through the door.

He shook his head as he thought about the miracle of coincidence while steering the truck back to 239 Grouse Road. The first thing he would do is bring the trunk downstairs for easy access. Dora would love to go through it, looking for treasures to be used in the house. Likely, the trunk would end up in the house on display somewhere. It could be a place to store quilts for guests to wrap themselves on cold evenings while sitting on the porch enjoying a cup of their favorite hot beverage. The repeated filigree pattern seemed to be a perfect way to honor the original builders of Brooks and would look great in their advertising. And, later, Len would do his own google search about *bearer bonds*.

He was getting the old trunk down the attic stairs when he heard the front door open.

"Grant, it's Lowry yur nabor. Can I come in?"

Len recognized the grizzled voice of his neighbor Ernie Lowry. Ernie lived a little down the road and frequently found his way to Brooks, usually pulling his wagon. His daily routine included patrolling the well-traveled road beyond Brooks in search of treasures discarded by litterbugs. He was a wood carver and looked almost as twisted and gnarled as the walking stick he leaned on.

"Is that you, Ernie? I'm upstairs. Give me a minute."

Len hoisted the trunk using the rope handles and proceeded down the hall toward the staircase.

Ernie hobbled forward, and Len noticed his eyes zero in on the trunk.

"Watcha got there, Len?"

Len put the trunk down and grabbed an empty cardboard box near the entryway. He started transferring the contents. "I found this trunk in the attic. I'll take everything home so Dora and I can go through it and see what we can salvage. I want to make a memory wall so our guests can know where this old place has been."

"Ah, that's a dandy idea. That's some mighty fine-lookin' wood ya got there, boy. It looks like it needs a little tender lovin' care, though. I'd sure nuf'd like to get m'hands on it."

The older man reverently approached the trunk and gently traced the spirals of the filigree pattern with his arthritic fingers. He leaned into the coffer, closed his eyes, and breathed deeply. "Peple dun't fully preciate lumber. Me, I like the way it smells. I can tell ya what kind of tree a wood comes from just by its smell." The older man's chin jutted out confidently as he stomped his walking stick against the floor.

Brooks' hardwood floor accepted the thump and recognized the woodsman as a master; anticipation filled his frame.

Len felt a kindred spirit with this older man. It was evident that Lowry's rapport with wood was akin to what Len felt with nature.

"Ernie, I have an idea. Why don't you take this trunk and clean it up for me? I'd be happy to pay you for your time. It would look great here in the house where people could enjoy it. Do you have time to do that?"

"Ya kiddin', I'll make time to spend with this beauty. I got m'wagon just outside. Ya help me put it in there, and I'll take er home and get busy on er."

"I'll do better than that. I'll put it and your wagon in the back of my truck, and I'll drive you home and help you get it into your shop."

"Ya got yursef a deal, and I don't want no pay. Maybe that purty wife a yurs'll invite me to yur first dinner in this ol' place."

Len smiled and put his arm on Ernie's shoulders.

"I think I can arrange that, for sure."

Len lifted the trunk and proceeded out the door with Lowry trailing behind.

"Call me when you finish with the trunk, and I'll pick it up. I'll bet Dora will want to put it near the front entry. It's too beautiful to be hidden away in a corner."

"Oh sure, it'll probly take me a few days. Once I git goin' on somethin' like this, I can't stop til it's finished. I'm gonna clean up those rope hinges, too. It's gonna look good. Ya wait 'n see."

As Len pulled out of the driveway, the familiar truck belonging to his son rounded the corner. They pulled parallel and greeted one another with similar wide grins.

"Hey, son, I'll be right back. Ernie's going to do a wood project for me so I'm taking him back to his place."

"Okay. Hi, Mr. Lowry. How are you doing these days?"

"Well, youngin', some say I'm gettin' old and cranky. I try to be nice, but sometimes m' mouth don't cooperate."

Len and Roger both joined the older man's cackly laughter.

Len said, "In the meantime, would you move that pile of wood scraps left from the benches we built? Stack it next to the outbuilding west of the house. I'll be using it for kindling in the fireplaces. Feel free to take what you want."

Roger nodded. "You take good care of yourself, Mr. Lowry. The world needs you. I'll get going on that wood, Dad."

"Thanks, son, I won't be long. I appreciate your help."

Len drove the older man and his cargo to an aged dwelling alongside an equally timeworn but amply fitted work shed. Len pulled the wagon carrying the trunk, while Ernie steadied it.

Inside the shed a talented artisan had tools stacked in the corners and hanging on the walls.

Len placed the trunk on the workbench as directed by Lowry, bid farewell, and returned to Brooks.

Len pulled into the property, and Roger waved at him, then opened the truck door for his father.

"Hi, Dad."

"Nice work, Roger, you've made a lot of progress in a short amount of time. I see you've about got that stack of wood cleaned up."

"Yeah, it was just odd-sized pieces. Besides," and he grinned, "I've always wanted to be like you, Dad, hardworking and compassionate."

Len laughed. "I'd say you're already there."

Roger put his arm across his dad's shoulders. "Are you ready to start placing those benches?"

"Yup, and once we're finished, Brooks will be that much closer to opening for business." He held his right hand with his thumb and pointer finger open a few inches and peeked through the space. "With a few exceptions."

The quiet splendor surrounded them as the afternoon sun dug its way through the varied hues of nature. Len and Roger occupied front-row seats in Brooks' concert hall with the bonus of surround sound. Coos from mourning doves and caws of crows communed with the environment. Various bird chirps came from the orchestra pit and intermingled in a refrain of nature's chorus. This enormous cast followed the lead of the baton held by the grand maestro, Mother Nature.

Father and son exchanged a knowing glance, then Len said, "Daylight's a burning, Roger, let's get a move on. I've made a map and I know just where I want the benches."

They loaded the five benches in the truck, and the two men drove through the forest using the utility trail they had blazed over the last several months.

To prevent further damage to the old map he had found, Len drew a new one, marking the five stations with x's. Each area was dedicated to one of the five senses. When Len initially investigated the property using the original map, he acknowledged the spiritual influence he felt with each space.

The first bench was for sight. Len had found a gazing ball in one of the outbuildings and placed it where rays of sunshine shot through tree branches. The ball gave visual evidence of all-encompassing love from a higher source, reflecting images of the forest. Perhaps, even blind people could sense nature at this station.

The second stop was near a small stream and dedicated to hearing. It was an invitation to seek clarity in every bird call, every gurgle of stream, every whisper of wind, and every crackle of a leaf. There was evidence of peace, spirituality, hope, renewal, transformation, and love, all within the confines of what some might call silence.

Len's favorite sensory station was off the beaten path. A place with bountiful plant life where the water rippled as it bounced over shiny rocks and pebbles. When it rained, pellets landed with a resounding *kerplunk* and joined the swirling. This was for smell. Unpleasant smells were welcomed and blended with nature.

The fourth bench was placed near the herb and working gardens. Taste was teased when soft breezes brought sweet smells from the fruit orchard. Here, the open kitchen window would dispatch the aromas of a delectable meal.

The last bench represented touch and was set near Brooks' back entry in the middle of a lush grass area. A nearby stream invited bare feet to caress the smooth rocks or become enlivened with the cool, moving water.

With the last bench in place, Len stepped away and openly admired the fruits of his labors.

"That's it, Roger, we're done."

"It looks good, Dad. I envy what you've created here. Great-grandpa Grant would be proud to see how you've brought this place back to life. It's more than just an old house, it has character. I can feel something intangible here. I love that it's part of my history."

"I'm glad to hear you feel that way—it'll belong to you and your sisters someday. It's more than a house to me too. It seems to be living. I talk to it like an old friend sometimes. I swear it communicates with me on a level I can't explain."

Len took a deep breath, closed his eyes, and felt at peace with his decision to revive Brooks.

"We'd better go. Your mother said Robyn is calling tonight. I'm sure your mom has fixed a special meal for you. Bring your truck around. I'll lock the back door, and we'll be off for the day."

"Okay, I'm looking forward to talking to Robyn and Mom's cooking. See you at home."

When Len reached the front door, he saw the cardboard box. He tossed the envelope holding the safety deposit box key into the box. That would remind Dora to go to the bank and sign the new signature card. He also included the envelope with the maps for bench placement. He taped the box closed, set it near the front door, and remembered he had opened a kitchen window. He heard Roger's car horn as he walked back to close it.

"Dad, you okay?"

Len called back, "Yeah, I'm fine, be there in a few."

Len closed the kitchen window and hurried out the front door—without the box.

Take risks but keep your boots on the ground.

Roger laid his napkin next to his plate, leaned back in his chair, and folded his hands across his midsection.

"Mom, that was a first-rate meal. Thanks, your home cooking hit the spot."

"I love making my men smile. A full belly usually does the trick. We both appreciate you making the trip to help your dad. He loves that tool belt you gave him."

"If you want, Mom, I could have one made especially for you. Maybe I could get Grandma Eva to bedazzle it for you."

Dora stopped mid-stride at the sink. "Boy, that would be a sight, wouldn't it? Grandma Eva with her glue guns and glitter."

"I'll drop in on her tomorrow morning before I leave town. How's Grams doing anyway?"

"She's doing fine. I talked to her doctor a week ago, and he said she's in great shape," said Mom.

"Ann sent a basket of handicraft items she gathered from her mom's place. I told her I'd be sure to get it to Grams before I came back."

"She seems to be enjoying life at the assisted living center. She's unofficially in charge of some of their activities and keeps her housemates busy. Her stamina amazes me."

After Roger helped to clean the remnants of their meal, he held his mother by the shoulders and kissed her forehead. "If you'll excuse me, I think I'll go to my room. I have some work to do for an inventory of the store." He started to walk away but stopped and turned around. "Dad, remind me again what's left to be done at Brooks?"

Len didn't respond immediately.

"The biggest job is clearing that area at the turnoff by that old sugar maple tree. We need a better view of oncoming traffic, it's a safety issue. Beyond that, I've made a drawing for some house and garden lighting, and then, of course, there's the matter of stocking the place." He stopped for a second. "Blazes, I forgot that stuff I found in the attic. I put the box by the front door, so I'd see it on the way out, and I still forgot it."

Dora put her hand on Len's shoulder. "Len, it's okay, don't worry about it. You've been running non-stop since early this morning. You're probably tired."

Len took the silverware from her hand and placed it in the drawer.

"Dora, I'm fine. I'm strong as an ox. I can keep up with the best of them, can't I, Roger?"

"Yes, Dad, you're a tough one, that's for sure. But Mom's right. You deserve some rest, and knowing you're so close to the finish line is good to hear. Why don't you take a few days to rest up and put Brooks on the back burner? Make a list of what's left to do, and I'll plan on coming back next weekend to knock them all out."

Len was silent for a few seconds, then he said, "You know, I think you're right. I'll spend a few days with my best girl and look forward to spending the weekend with my favorite son."

"Great! Mom, Ann has some ideas for your open house. I'll bring her back this weekend, and she can pitch those to you."

"I'd love to hear her ideas. I've been working on some things too, but I'll consider a fresh point of view."

"Great, I'm going to get busy with my inventory. I'll see you both in the morning, goodnight."

"Night, son," they both said in unison.

"Len, let's sit down, and you can tell me more about the box," said Dora.

"Good idea, my love. It's stuff I found in an old trunk in the attic. Ernie Lowry showed up when I was toting it downstairs and got excited about it needing some TLC. I emptied the trunk and put everything in a cardboard box. We could go through it and see if there's anything there we could use."

"Oh, that does sound fun, go on."

"Well, except for a quilt top, it's mostly odds and ends. User manuals for small appliances, blueprints for Brooks, I think, and a smaller wooden box of some family stuff. I saw trinkets, an old tintype picture, and a leather-bound notebook."

"A quilt top? That sounds intriguing."

Dora finished wiping down the counter and sat beside her husband, reclining in her chair. They smiled at one another and clasped hands as Dora closed her eyes.

"Dora, I almost forgot. I stopped in at the bank today, and guess who's working there?"

"Don't make me guess. Who did you see?"

"Robyn's friend, Myla. She says she's been there almost a year. She asked that we give her best to Robyn. She said she'd email our girl and get the lowdown on Australia. Said to tell you hello too and that she wants to come to Brooks when we have our grand opening."

"Why were you at the bank?"

"Oh, that's the part I forgot to tell you. I decided to get a bigger safety deposit box. We've got papers regarding the whole probate thing on Brooks, and I didn't want to stuff them in the small box. Anyway, Myla helped me get a bigger box, and you need to sign the signature card."

"Does it have to be done right away?"

"No, but don't wait too long."

Len and Dora got comfortable and would probably have dozed were it not for the unrelenting sound of a croaking frog. Len and Dora sat up in complete surprise and stared wide-eyed at one another.

Roger came out of his room laughing. "Mom, Dad, I think that's your computer calling. Let me get it before they leapfrog away."

"Len, I almost forgot about Australia. The kids are calling. It's tomorrow morning there."

Dora abandoned her chair and hurried toward the office. Len got up a little slower. "Dora, why does our computer sound like a frog?"

Roger got to the computer and answered the call. When he did, the face of his youngest sister, surrounded by tiny humans, filled the screen.

"Hi, Robyn, you look great. Hey, Rachel, Lizzie. You girls get prettier every time I see you," said Roger.

"Hi, Uncle Roger. Today, I'm seven years old," said Rachel.

"I heard that, happy birthday. Did your mom make you a cake?"

"Yes!"

"Well, I have to tell you something."

"What?"

Roger leaned closer to the screen. "You're missing your two front teeth. What happened?"

"Oh, Uncle Roger, you're teasing me."

"Yes, I am. You are the cutest little girl ever, even without your two front teeth."

"Uncle Roger, I have my teeth," said five-year-old Lizzie.

"You sure do, and you are as pretty as ever. I love both of you girls. Where's little Lenny?"

Robyn lifted Lenny to her lap. A grin enveloped a captivating bubble of saliva as it formed from his mouth, and Robyn wiped it away with a tissue. Lenny's arms and hands flailed, trying to grab hold of the computer screen.

"Hi, Lenny, how's our big boy doing?" asked Roger.

Lenny looked up at his mother and then craned his neck, looking at his sisters.

Robyn whispered, "Lenny, that's Uncle Roger. He's at Grammy and Grampy's house. Say, hi, Uncle Roger."

"Where's Grumpy?" asked Lenny.

Roger laughed. "Just a minute, Lenny, Grammy and Grampy are right here."

Roger gave up the office chair for his father and brought a chair for his mother. He peeked over their shoulders to bid farewell.

"I'm leaving, kiddos, but we'll talk another time. Have a great birthday, Rachel. I love you all. I'll tell Aunt Ann and your cousins that I saw you. Bye."

"Bye," they all chorused.

The phone call ended thirty minutes later, and Len rapped on Roger's bedroom door.

"Come in," called Roger.

Len poked his head through the opening.

"You decent? I have a question."

"Yeah, Dad, I'm still working on this inventory list. What's up?"

Len opened the door.

"Roger, why does our computer sound like a frog?" asked Len.

Roger laughed. "I think I know what happened. When we set up that video program for you, Luke and Devon, your clever grandsons, offered to help. I heard them tittering and trying different sounds for your video notifications, but I didn't think much about it. I should have because what one doesn't think of the other does, and I've learned through the years they'll always be one step ahead of me. Anyway, I'm pretty sure they decided to surprise you with croaking frogs, and they'll be pleased to know their senses of humor have been duly noted."

"Oh, I see—those little pranksters. I'll have to give some serious thought regarding their comeuppance."

Roger laughed. "Night, Dad."

"Good night, son."

5

Family is the most precious gift you'll ever have.
Cherish your loved ones, and always make time for them.

Brooks heard about adding benches in the forest from a wind current, and he approved. The five spots had always held a special reverence. It would be nice to have mortals enjoying them again. Throughout the many years of his existence, he soaked up conversations, witnessed the trials and tribulations of his residents, learned about sarcasm, and circulated chortles of merriment through his pipes. He remembered one called Beth as his first caretaker. She polished his floors, dusted his ledges, and washed his windows while she sang. Her lovely voice rang through his rafters in perfect pitch. And now, she was one of the souls in his archives.

Through the many years, mortals often entered his grounds uninvited, and Brooks was not opposed to having fun with them. He often played jokes on them. He thought they would play back but ran off in fright instead. He vowed that this time, he would behave because, according to the rumor mill, these mortals were staying. Brooks heard the couple call him Brooks' Bed & Breakfast. He hoped they didn't plan on changing his name. It was much too long. He decided he would wait and see. After all, he had always been willing to learn new skills, and if it meant having people within his walls again, he was all in.

    He looked good these days. He had a new veneer of pale yellow, and his eaves were now white. The brick chimneys atop his new slate gray roof were neatly stacked with fresh red rock mortar. His hardwood floors gleamed with fresh varnish, kitchen cabinets sparkled with a new coat of paint, and new weather stripping joined the family. The original float glass windows dazzled in their new frames, and chandeliers sparkled in all their finery.

6

Work hard and honest, like the sweat on a farmer's brow.

A STERN-LOOKING WOMAN sat the front desk of the law office. "Good morning, sir. Do you have an appointment?"

"Yes, I'm Len Grant. I'm scheduled to see Mr. Karvelas."

"Have a seat, Mr. Grant, let me see if he's ready for you."

Len sat in the empty waiting room and picked up a magazine from the coffee table. He held open the magazine but didn't look at the pages as he studied his surroundings. The room was sterile, stern, solemn, like the woman who greeted him.

Her face looked stretched like a canvas, and her mouth was swollen and misshapen. Her hair was pulled back tightly at the nape of her neck, and she wore diamond stud earrings. The ring on her hand was a little gaudy for Len's tastes. The nameplate on her desk identified her in bold block letters as *Penelope A. Davis, Paralegal.*

"I should have encouraged my girls to become paralegals," he murmured.

The pristine glass desktop of Ms. Davis's clutter-free mahogany desk was spotless. A calendar notebook lay open to the current date, and a Parker Ballpoint Pen rested in the seam. The office chair looked comfortable and very expensive. The only adornment was a vase filled with spring blooms prominently sitting at the front corner. The room was well-lit with overhead lighting, but floor lamps were also in the seating area. Soft piano music played in the background.

Suddenly, Len felt out of place. He stood, straightened his trousers, and adjusted the collar of his sports shirt. He ran his fingers through his hair and started to sit back down.

Ms. Davis opened the door of Karvelas's office.

"Mr. Grant, Mr. Karvelas will see you now." She seemed like she was trying to smile, but her frozen face couldn't quite manage the movement.

"Thanks," said Len as he moved toward the open door.

The woman held the door for their client, and when he entered, he was greeted by a jovial-looking man ready to shake hands. He said, "That'll be all Penny. Have a seat, Mr. Grant, and let's get acquainted before we figure out how I can help you."

Len took a seat in a chair opposite the attorney's desk.

"Penny, hold up a minute, please," said Mr. Karvelas. "Mr. Grant, would you like coffee, soda, or water? I'm parched and would like a Diet Coke. How about you?"

"Maybe a ginger ale?"

"Penny, be a doll and bring us a Coke and a ginger ale. Also, Sarah sent in a loaf of zucchini bread. Slice that up, put a few on a dish for us, and don't forget some napkins."

Ms. Davis closed the door, mumbling as she entered an adjoining room with a small kitchen outfitted with a refrigerator and microwave.

"I'm not 'doll,' you oaf. I'm Ms. Davis. Why can't you get that through your misogynistic head? We need proper decorum. We're a law office, not a snack bar."

She scolded herself yet again at having to work for her brother-in-law. Her sister got her this job six months ago when she needed it most, and she'd hated it ever since. She promised herself again that when she made it big, she would leave this sloppy place and her self-important sister in the dust. It was only a matter of time before she figured out a way to live as she deserved, and that wouldn't be fetching sodas and cookies.

She took a tray from the cupboard, filled two glasses with ice, poured soda into each glass, put the bread on a plate, and grabbed a few napkins. The soda cans were placed on the tray, and she returned to her boss's office.

Before entering, she rapped on the door lightly and waited for Mr. Big Shot to beckon her in.

Len was seated in the chair front and center of Karvelas's desk, which, as usual, was littered with stacks of files and sticky notes galore. How he kept everything straight, she didn't understand. Her stomach roiled every time she came into the office. His rumpled suit and messy hair completed the whole unkept scene. Despite it all, he was known as the best lawyer for miles around. People loved him and depended on his expertise. His business was consistent, and his lifestyle reflected his success. Her sister had a beautiful home and well-behaved children, and the family took frequent vacations. Once more, Penelope Davis shook her head at the unfairness of life.

Penny stepped back into the office and put the tray on the only available space on the desk. "Will that be all, Mr. Karvelas?"

She pronounced each word with preciseness accompanied by a noticeable glare.

Jake Karvelas didn't seem to notice the look of disdain and didn't seem affected by her tone.

"I need that brief on the Alexander case this afternoon, so be sure it's ready. Thanks for the refreshments, though. I'll buzz you if I think of anything else."

Ms. Davis turned and left the room, closing the door behind her. She took the Alexander file from the cabinet, slammed the drawer shut, and returned to her desk, her grimacing mouth firmly in place.

"Mr. Grant, what can I do for you today?"

"First of all, thanks for making time for me. When I called, your girl said you couldn't fit me in for two weeks. I hope my insistence on something more immediate hasn't been too much of a bother."

"Nonsense, Penny sometimes has illusions of my grandeur. Let's focus on what brings you here today, and please call me Jake."

"I'll make it quick. I know you're busy."

Karvelas extended the plate of zucchini bread to Len.

"Help yourself. This is better than anything you'll find at the best bakery anywhere."

Len sipped the ginger ale and then took a bite of the bread. He smacked his lips in approval. "Wow, that is good. Your wife needs to go into the business."

"I told you."

Len took a few moments to collect his thoughts, then wiped his mouth with the napkin. "What do you know about bearer bonds? I recently found some, and I need someone to tell me whether they have value, and if they do, tell me how to cash them in."

"Bearer bonds, hmm."

Karvelas pulled a book from the shelf behind his desk and flipped through the pages. He settled on a page and used his finger to trace the words he read out loud.

> "A bearer bond is a debt security not registered to a specific owner, allowing anyone possessing the bond to claim ownership and receive interest payments. They've been used since the 1800s by governments and corporations as a convenient way to raise capital. Due to tax evasion and money laundering concerns, their popularity declined in the late 20th century. They offer anonymity and easy transferability, making them attractive to some investors. However, they carry increased risks, such as loss or theft, and are subject to stricter regulatory scrutiny."

Len's hands lay in his lap throughout the attorney's wordy explanation. In nervous anticipation, his thumb traced a continuous circle on the knuckle of his opposing thumb. He was absorbed in that action throughout Jake's monologue.

Jake looked up.

Len stopped the nervous fidget and met Karvelas's eyes. "I took a picture of one of the bonds with my phone. Could you check it out for me?" Len pulled out his phone and pushed several buttons to bring the picture to the forefront. He handed the phone to Karvelas.

Jake enlarged the shot and took his time studying the picture.

"I'll check this out. Don't get your hopes up, Len. Bearer bonds have been outlawed in the United States since the 1980s due to their association with illegal activities. However, if I remember right, some bearer bonds can still be redeemed if the issuer exists. According to what I see here, these bonds were issued in 1925. I'll look into the issuer's status and get back to you. Are they in a secure location?"

"Yes, I've put them in my safety deposit box in the bank. My wife and I are the only ones with authority to access it."

"Great, until we know their value, keep them under lock and key. They belong to whoever has possession. They're like cash. Do you have any other questions for me?"

"No, but my insides are jumping all over the place just thinking about how all this could change mine and my wife's lives."

"I hope it works out positively, Len. I love seeing good people enjoy the bounties of life. But for now, I need you to email that picture to this address."

Jake handed Len a business card. "Be sure Penny has your phone number so I can get back to you as soon as I have any word."

"What do I owe you for all this?"

Jake stood and the two men shook hands.

"Today's visit is complimentary, but fees will be attached to the time we spend on the case from this point on. I bill at two hundred and fifty dollars per hour, and we do invoices monthly. That fee applies no matter the result of my investigation. This seems straightforward, but if it's more complex, I'll let you know, and you can decide how far you want to go with further work. I first need to determine whether the issuing company is still in business and how they've previously addressed outstanding bearer bonds. It's hard to guess, but I'm a fair man, Len, and I won't dawdle. Every case I take, I handle quickly and equitably."

Jake opened the office door. "I hope this works out for both of us. If those bonds are as valuable as we hope, you'll need a good attorney to help you with financial planning. If you need help emailing that picture, ask Penny to assist you."

"No, I'm fine. This new technology is confusing sometimes, but I've figured out a lot of it, I can do this. Thanks again for your time."

Jake walked with Len to the elevator.

He waited as it closed, and then directed his attention toward Ms. Penelope Davis.

"Penny, Mr. Grant will email us a document I need for further investigation. Please make a copy and put it on my desk as soon as it arrives. How are you coming with that brief?"

"It'll be ready in about fifteen minutes." She stopped typing and, with exasperation, turned toward her boss.

"Jake, I've often asked you not to call me Penny, especially in the office. My name is Penelope, and I'm your paralegal, not a waitress. I don't like being treated like a carhop."

"First of all, 'Penelope,' we both know you are not a paralegal. I've not said anything about your using that title. You don't have a degree or certification and are not a paralegal. I've known you since you were a teenager named Penny. That's how I was first introduced to you. I don't mean disrespect, but you'll always be Penny to me. As far as treating you like a carhop, I need my clients to feel at home while they're here, and if that means giving them refreshments, I expect you to help with that because we're a two-person office. I'm swamped, and I need you to handle the paperwork and help me make our clients comfortable. However,

I will try harder to refer to you as Ms. Davis while we're in the office to show mutual respect."

Karvelas took a deep breath and decided to mend a fence or two.

"Penny, Ms. Davis, you have this job because your sister wants to look after you. I genuinely appreciate what you do. If you want a different job with more responsibility, get an education. I'm not fanning the flames of your false perceptions. We've had this discussion more than once. Please do your job. I promise to be more sensitive to your feelings."

Jake went back into his office, closing the door firmly behind him.

Once again, Penelope Davis had been put in her place and reminded of her low status as a thirty-year-old typist for her brother-in-law.

7

Never stop learning. Stay curious about the world around you, and never be afraid to ask questions.

Penny Davis's apartment comprised a small part of the basement in her sister's home. It was part of the deal, "to help her get back on her feet," that Sarah offered six months prior. After a long series of bad relationships, a dysfunctional lifestyle, and dead-end jobs, Sarah took pity on her younger sister. She convinced her attorney husband to give her a job. Big sister then invited little sister to live in the renovated basement of the Karvelas' home. Sarah hoped it would provide Penny time to reset her life.

Later that day, Penny entered her apartment through the back entrance and descended the stairs. If only there were a separate entrance so she didn't have to trek past kids and her keepers, but it was free, and heaven knew that was all she could afford. If she ever got her credit cards paid off, she would get off the dole of these people.

"Penny, is that you?"

"Yes, Sarah, it's me."

Sarah poked her head around the corner and greeted her sibling with a big smile that was acknowledged by a begrudging nod.

"How was your day? Jake hasn't checked in with me. You guys must have been super busy."

"Yes, we were. My fingers ache. I typed all day long."

"Hey, Penny, it's the weekend, what do you have planned?"

"Nothing, and don't take that to mean I want to go out with your newest find. I'm going to stay home and catch up on some reading."

"Well, I do have someone I want you to meet. This man has a good business and is very nice. I told him about you, and he said he'd like to meet you. He suggested having lunch together tomorrow. That would give you the chance to see for yourself. I've known him for a while. He's done some work for us. I even checked him out, and I don't know why he hasn't been snatched up before now."

"Sarah, why can't you let me find my own friends? I think it's pathetic getting set up like this, and our taste in men is very different."

"You say you want someone who can take care of you, who isn't afraid of hard work, someone who'll respect and love you. I think this guy would be a good father, too."

"Sarah, I'm not interested in being a mother to whiney kids. I'm probably too old for that gig anyway."

Penny felt an uncomfortable stare from her sister and relentingly said, "Okay, tell me more about him."

"Well, he's probably about your age, has never been married, has no kids, has his own home, and has a great personality. He's fun to talk to."

"Where did you meet him, and what kind of work does he do?"

"He's a plumber, Penny, and is well sought after in the community. Plumbers make a lot of money. I drove past his home, and it's nice."

Penny's persona was deflated with contradictions between her private life and public image.

"You want me to consider being socially active with a plumber? Let's explore this a little more, Sarah. Tell me, how tall is this man hunk, and how much does he weigh?"

"He's a plumber, Penny. They need a lot of upper body strength to do that kind of work." Sarah shrugged her shoulders. "He's about your height, and he's stout."

"Does he have any hair on his head, Sarah?"

Sarah hesitated momentarily and answered, "Truthfully, I don't know. He's always worn a hat when I've talked to him."

"Look at me, Sarah. Do you honestly think I'm looking to be tied up to a fat, bald man about my height? If I were looking for male companionship, it would be with someone who turns heads, not pipe wrenches."

Penny took a couple more descending stairs and stopped.

"Honestly, Sarah, maybe I don't want any man. Maybe I'd rather be by myself. Just because you enjoy being Miss Suzy Homemaker with your perfect life doesn't mean it's right for me."

Penny stomped down the remaining stairs as her words trailed off.

"I'll have dinner ready in about an hour if you'd like to join us," said Sarah, still sounding upbeat.

The door to the basement apartment answered with a heavy slam.

Penny kicked off her shoes and went to her bedroom. She changed into a pair of sweats and a T-shirt. Walking barefoot back to the combination living room/kitchen, Penny opened the Moroccan leather briefcase she carried back and forth to work. It cost a bundle, and she thought it worth every dollar she spent. Its pungent tannery fragrance made her feel heady, as did the attention she got from others. It fed her inflated ego, and she felt nothing like a typist in its company. It's one of the reasons her credit cards carried a carry-over balance every month. She lived by the adage, *Dress for the job you want, not the job you have.*

Her closet was replete with designer labels. She ensured her shoes reflected that same fashion tone. She sought the services of the finest aesthetician to keep her skin looking like porcelain, and these days, that meant chemical peels and Botox, and yeah, it was expensive, so what?

By swallowing her pride and groveling with her sister and brother-in-law, Penelope Davis managed to stay in their good graces and avoid incurring additional living expenses. She forlornly complained to herself that she barely earned enough money to take care of her personal needs, period.

With a deep sigh, she sifted through the contents of her briefcase and removed the extra copy she had made from Mr. Grant's email to satisfy her curiosity. She convinced herself that knowing the intimate details of all cases was part of her job, and she studied the document. It was something called a bearer bond and appeared to be issued in 1925 by a company called "Pead Semiconductors."

Penny googled the business but didn't find anything. She googled "bearer bonds" and gasped with each discovery while reading a two-page summary. She sat up and leaned forward, rereading the entire article, stopping at the part that said,

> "Bearer bonds are easily transferable, easily negotiable and anonymous, and in certain circumstances, they have distinct advantages over other forms of currency, such as cash."

Penny sat deep in thought at the information in her hands. She put the document back in her briefcase, donned a pair of house shoes, and padded up the stairs to have dinner with her precious family, realizing it was in her best interest to seek forgiveness for the earlier exchange. She would eat a little crow and consent to meeting the plumber and even go out with Mr. Butt Crack, but she already knew she wouldn't like him.

8

Invest in relationships, like tending a fruitful garden.

Jake Karvelas practically burst out of the elevator. His research about the bearer bonds was the reason behind his exuberance. He was excited to share his findings about life-changing news with his new client, Len Grant. In times like this, Jake found his law career to be the most fulfilling.

"Good morning, Ms. Davis, please get Len Grant on the phone."

Penny was all ears. She had done her research and was sure she knew the source of her brother-in-law's enthusiasm.

"Yes, I'll get him right away, Mr. Karvelas."

Jake didn't break his stride as he entered his office, removed his coat, and set his tattered old briefcase on the cluttered desk.

Meanwhile, at Brooks, Len's phone rang as he lay on the floor beneath the desk in the library. The desk's center drawer groaned in protest whenever it was opened or closed. Len was determined to rectify the problem while sprawled on his back with tools and lubricant ready. He answered the call while in that position.

The intercom buzzed in the law office as Jake opened his briefcase. He jabbed the button to connect to Penny, knowing it was about his call to Grant.

"Yeah, Penny, did you get him?"

"Of course, he's on line one."

"Good, go ahead and put him through."

Penelope's headset was muted, and she became an invisible part of the conversation. She had done this many times throughout her employment history. She convinced herself she needed to know the nuts and bolts of the businesses she worked for. It helped her to be a more valued employee, she reasoned. Besides that, it was usually very entertaining.

"Len, do you have time to come in today? I've some great news about your bearer bonds and don't want to discuss it over the phone. We need to set some things in motion."

"Yeah, I can come in today."

"Great, I have court in a half hour, and it'll likely last a few hours. Drop in about one this afternoon. I'll have an hour or so, and we can hammer this out. We need to jump some hurdles, but it's easier than I thought. You, my friend, are a fortunate man."

"Thanks, Jake. I'll see you in a few hours."

Len gathered his tools, got up from the floor, and sat heavily in the imposing desk chair. He shivered at the implications of the short conversation, and his mind raced with possibilities. He leaned back and closed his eyes, listening to piano music from hidden speakers.

"Love Me Tender," "Unchained Melody," "Autumn Leaves."

The music brought up images of Dora and the love he had felt for her since they first met as teenagers. From the day they pledged their love across the altar, she had been the rock of their home, and he knew himself to be the luckiest man on earth to have her heart. He was confident that Dora would support the work they could do to change other people's lives with whatever the value the bearer bonds ended up being.

The melody of "Love is a Many Splendored Thing" hauntingly filled the room, and again, images of Dora flooded his brain. This was a song they both felt belonged to their love story. He opened the desk drawer, removed writing paper and a pencil, and titled the top of the paper, "BG."

An hour later, he folded the prose-filled sheet and put it in his pocket. He would add it to his notebook later. Dora was his "BG" — his "Best Girl."

Everything in the library absorbed the words zinging through the air, inspiring the writing of the man called Len. The books on the shelves strained to share their words of influence.

Brooks remembered that many years ago, Len's great-grandfather, Tim Grant, found a rock in a stream in the forest of Brooks. It glimmered in the morning sun when the water bounced across it. He retrieved the rock and caressed its heart shape with his thumb. He decided that with some work, it would be the perfect gift for his wife, Beth. He spent many hours polishing the rock to a high sheen, and after etching her initials BG onto the stone, he crafted an aluminum wire-like basket for it and suspended it from a silver chain. He presented it to her for her birthday, and she wore it around her neck for the rest of her life.

Len arrived at Karvelas Law Offices with five minutes to spare. He entered with trepidation, knowing he had to deal with Ms. Davis' arrogance. Instead, when the elevator doors opened, the haughty woman from the week before greeted him with a slightly strained smile.

"Well, good afternoon, Mr. Grant. So good to see you again."

She rose from her chair and rounded her desk. "Mr. Karvelas said to bring you in as soon as you arrived." She led him to the office door, rapped softly, and held the door open, gesturing to him to precede her.

"Mr. Grant, Mr. Karvelas, can I get you anything? I stocked up on ginger ale, and when I found out we were expecting you this afternoon, Mr. Grant, I made a special trip to the local bakery and picked up some shortbread."

"Uh, okay, sure. I'll have a ginger ale, thanks."

"Ms. Davis," said Karvelas, "I'll have the usual, and the shortbread sounds good, but I haven't had lunch, and I'm starving."

"What about you, Mr. Grant? Are you hungry? I'd be glad to order in for both of you."

"That's a good idea," said Jake. "There's a place around the corner that makes the best hamburgers I've ever had. Are you in the mood for a burger?"

"Sure, I could use lunch."

Again, Penny seemed to don her *nice* attitude. "Any special requests for how the burgers are cooked?"

"Not for me, Ms. Davis. I pretty much like everything," said Len.

Jake added, "You know me, I want it rare with all the fixin's."

"Sure, I'll get that ordered and bring it in when it arrives."

Penelope exited the room, went to her desk, ordered lunch, and set herself up to listen to the conversation behind closed doors.

Karvelas motioned for his guest to be seated at a small table in the corner of the office. "This will be more comfortable than eating off the corner of my desk. You're going to love the deli Penny is getting lunch from. It's one of my favorite places."

Jake patted his paunch and then rested his hand on the single file lying on the table. "I have your file."

"Thanks. I'm looking forward to getting some answers."

Jake Karvelas sat down and immediately picked up the brown manila folder. He removed a handful of papers highlighted with yellow markings. He thumbed through the documents using his sausage-like pointer finger, stopping briefly here and there as though reminding himself of various passages. He reached the last page and went through the same action from top to bottom, then abruptly allowed the pages to fall back in place, tapped his hand on the whole package, and looked up at Len with an unabashed grin.

"Len, by all indications, you will be a wealthy man. The bonds you have were issued by Pead Semiconductors in 1925. They were part of a successful attempt to raise funds to finance an up-and-coming research and development company on the very brink of the IT industry we have today. Pead made a lot of progress in that industry and enjoyed moderate success. We don't know how many of these bonds are still around. Still, the company that bought out Pead Semiconductors is aware of them. They're prepared to pay the bearer of said bonds handsomely in exchange for them. These bonds were called in years ago, but since there has never been registration information, there was no way to notify the holders officially. Despite that, you are entitled to a portion of their face value by the original call feature of the bond."

Len sighed and leaned back in his chair, extending his long legs, and hanging on to the chair arms as if preparing himself for a rocket ride.

"This is unreal," he choked.

"I'm not finished. Bearer bonds aren't used anymore. In the early fifties, the government realized that such bonds had been misused to cover up criminal activity or circumvent the law. As a result, US-issued bonds became nearly extinct, and payment became uncertain even for those still in existence. There are only a few banking agents that will cash your coupons."

"I figured there had to be a catch. So, please give it to me straight. Jake, you said I was going to be a rich man. How rich, and what kind of hoops do I have to jump through to see any of it? And how much will it cost me to make it all happen?"

"I've spoken with a banking agent who will cash these coupons. I was told they would need to be sent to a processing center and that doing the necessary paperwork would take some time. Even though interest payments stopped years ago, you are entitled to the original face value plus the interest accrued thirty years before the call date. Based on the information gleaned from the picture I sent them of the one bond, they have set things in motion. I'm registered as your agent at this point. They told me your bonds will easily bring you two and a half million dollars." Jake finished with a slap to the table.

The pair sat in silence, broken by a rap on the door.

"I have lunch here for you two, and it smells delicious. I hope you're both hungry."

Penny laid out the lunch like a mistress of the household. "Is there anything else I can do for either of you?"

"Len, do you need anything else?" asked Karvelas.

Len stared out the office window and silently shook his head.

"I think we're good with what's here," said Jake.

Penny left the office.

Len watched Jake attack the sandwich before him like a hungry lion pouncing on its prey, tearing it limb from limb. Len picked up his sandwich and took a bite.

He chewed quietly as he digested his thoughts, then swallowed, leaned on the table, and rested his slightly whiskered chin on his hand.

"Jake, let me review what you just said. I have a dozen bearer bonds, and there's a company willing to pay big bucks for them. You are listed as my agent with this company, so will we have some contract between us?"

"Of course, and you're right to be cautious." Jake took a yellow, legal-sized-lined notebook from the file on his desk and laid it before Len.

"I've already made some notes for a contract between us that will spell out my responsibility to you and how I expect this whole thing to play out. I'll have Ms. Davis prepare the contract, and she'll deliver it to you. I advise you to have it reviewed by another attorney of your choice. I'll have her include the contact information for the banking agent I've referenced today so you can personally contact them and ask any questions. If you're okay with everything in the contract, sign it and return it to Ms. Davis. She'll get it to our contact so they can move forward with the process. If, for some reason, you have any issue with the contract, just let us know, and we'll take care of it when I get back. In the meantime, keep your bonds under lock and key."

Len nodded. "Okay, but what do you mean when you get back."

"I'm scheduled to make a trip to Greece. It's my mother's eightieth birthday, and I've promised to take her to see her homeland. It'll be her first trip back since she left as a teenager. It means a lot to her, and I want to do it. I'll be gone almost three weeks."

Len sat up a little straighter with a look of annoyance.

"Look, I'll get everything started before I leave, and then it's a matter of waiting for the bureaucracy to clear their hoops. I'm told that'll take almost three weeks, just in time for me to finish it up when I return."

Len nodded. "Okay, I guess that'll work."

"Great, now tell me about the Brooks house. I've had a long-standing curiosity about that place. I understand it's been in your family for a long time."

"Yeah, it's been in probate for years, and I finally got a clear title a few months back. I've been renovating it so we can use it as a bed-and-breakfast. It's a remarkable piece of real estate."

"That's great, I'm happy for you. It sounds like an exciting life. This new money will be put to good use."

"Yes, but there's more, Jake. Dora and I have always been

involved in charity work in the community but in a modest way. My wife has a long list of things she sees in the community that must be addressed, especially for the underprivileged. She is one of the most generous, loving women you'll ever meet, and with extra money like this, she'll spend the rest of her life working for the good of others. She's roped our kids and me into multiple ventures, taking us out of our comfort zones. She would go to a meeting of some kind, and we all knew when she came home, there would be marching orders she would expect us to help with. This money will not be wasted, that's for sure. "

"She sounds like a very giving person."

Len smiled. "She is. I've leveraged everything for this house with the idea that it might create a source of income for us. I do believe in what I'm doing. I can't explain it, but something tells me that Dora and I were meant to fulfill some purpose with Brooks. I swear there are times when I feel that house is inspiring me." He chuckled. "Probably sounds kind of strange to you."

Jake didn't say anything. He was just listening and seemed to be interested in Len's explanation.

Len continued, "For example, there's something special about the library and its book-filled shelves. Brooks is much more than a bunch of lumber. It's a place where you feel safe and secure. I sense an insight when I'm there. It's like visiting a wise old grandparent."

"I'd like to see it one day."

"You will, of course. I grew up roaming those halls and playing hide-and-seek in the rooms. The forest surrounding it is magical, almost otherworldly. I can't explain it any better than that."

Len finished and sheepishly looked at the lawyer, who seemed mesmerized by Grant's tranquility and honesty.

"If this all works out, I'll surprise my wife with the news. Please keep all of this between us for now."

In the adjoining office, Penny sat immobilized by what she had just heard. She reached out and silenced her earphones, feeling a little daunted by the eavesdropping. Grant's description was more like he was talking about a person, not a house. She picked at the salad before her and sipped her flavored water. She was startled when she heard the doorknob and the increased volume of Jake Karvelas' boisterous voice.

The two men walked out of the office, and Jake said, "I will for sure, and it'll work out, Len."

"Enjoy Greece and show your mom a good time. Are you taking your family with you?"

"Indeed I am. The whole family is going. None of us has been there, and the kids are excited. My mom's been regaling us with stories about her childhood and has listed places she wants to show us. It'll be a trip to remember, I'm sure."

Len walked to the open doors of the elevator, turned, and waved. "Safe travels, Jake. See you when you get back."

Karvelas turned to his assistant. "Ms. Davis, I need you to come into my office for a few minutes. I have an important contract to go over with you. Please give it the highest priority for the balance of your day."

"I'm right behind you."

An hour later, Penny emerged from the office with her boss's hand-written pages and added instructions. It was for the eyes of Mr. Grant only, and it wasn't to be delivered to the client's home, nor was she to share it with anyone. She was to call the client on his cell phone and arrange a delivery place. It was all very hush-hush.

In truth, the fact that Jake was leaving in two days for his big fat Greek vacation reminded Penny that she was an outsider.

At home, she felt irritated toward the whole family. Every footstep she heard in her apartment from their domicile upstairs seemed to be stomping that feeling into her slighted heart.

Initially, she assumed she was part of the family going to Greece. It quickly became apparent that she would be left behind. She used subtle words to gain sympathy, but those subtleties were brushed aside.

9

Take a spell to listen up; Wisdom's often found in the quiet

Len intended to go home after the meeting with Karvelas but instead felt prompted to drive back to Brooks. As he drove, he couldn't help but think about the bonds and the changes in store if everything worked out. He pulled off the highway by the old sugar maple tree and onto the long driveway leading to Brooks, and then slowly rounded the bend, gravel crackled beneath the tires. As the circular driveway came into view, he noticed something he had never seen before, and he slammed on the brakes.

It was extraordinary. The driveway in front of the house resembled a smile. How had he missed it? All the times he had been in this spot. Len tipped his head to one side and then the other before driving forward a few more feet. He stopped, turned off the engine, and got out of the truck. He walked to the front and leaned against the hood. He found himself smiling back at Brooks.

It was like a beautiful landscape painting, finer than anything he had ever seen. Birds flew overhead, and the sun was on the horizon with a few fluffy white clouds scattered in the sky.

Branches of trees lifted their limbs in praise-like overtures above the old house's roof. A little dust devil resembling a toddler in a temper tantrum tried its best to wreak havoc in the side yard, abandoning the effort when ignored. He quietly enjoyed this piece of nature, reveling that it belonged to Dora and him.

He spoke almost to himself, "Dora and I have great plans for you. I hope I can see them through. I'm an old duffer, not as old as you, but I'm getting up there. I admit to preferring the old ways—I'm not comfortable with the fast pace of this world."

He took a deep breath, looked around, and he started thinking about his advancing years.

I get confused with technology, and most of the time, I don't even understand kids' language today. I wonder if I can keep up with your maintenance. I've accomplished a lot, but there's still much to do, and I know that running a bed-and-breakfast will be challenging. More than once, I've fallen to my knees begging for help. A friend once reminded me, "By small and simple things are great things brought to pass."

He looked up at the trees, and his thoughts began rambling again.

We're willing to count ourselves amongst those small and simple things, and we pray for guidance. You're going to have a lot of people meandering through here, and my goal is for people to find the motivation to take care of one another. You've been empty too long, and I feel sorry for a house without people.

Len did a three-hundred-and-sixty-degree turn, taking in the whole property, then he smiled again.

Thankfully, we're blessed to have Dora, I know she'll care for you, my friend. When I look at the changes in your rooms, I'm satisfied with her accomplishments. She's stronger and more capable than she realizes. She deserves so much more than I would ever have been able to give her on my own. If what I found in your attic is everything it looks to be, it will be a small start to giving my best girl everything she deserves, and I guess I have you to thank for that. You've kept those bonds safe and sound in your attic. And I've done a pretty good job with your grounds, too. Just look at you. You're over a century old but ageless.

Len walked over to some bushes where rocks protruded from the ground near them. He kicked at one of the rocks. It didn't budge. His mind mulled over some of the plans they had.

Sponsoring a kids' soccer team, wearing shirts with your name on the back. Barbeques of hot dogs and hamburgers, and the kids wandering the woods and splashing in the streams. Maybe an after-school activity for kids, community service projects to keep them busy doing worthwhile things for others. Maybe I'll teach classes about making a difference ecologically to protect our world, I like that idea.

He laughed out loud. "Things have been quiet here for many years. Are you up for some noise, Brooks?"

Len didn't expect an audible answer, of course, but he did notice a little breeze moving through the air and nodded his head in acknowledgment.

He was silent for a few moments, lost in thought.

If only your walls could talk. I have many questions about what you've been through with the families you've housed. For one thing, I would like to know my dad's antics as a boy. I have a feeling the hijinks of my twin grandsons could be rivaled.

Len chuckled, recalling a few instances of youthful mischief.

"I guess I had a few antics myself you could remind me about, right?" He paused. "Well, I better go. See you tomorrow."

Len got back in his truck and drove around the circular smile of the driveway and headed home.

Brooks looked on at the retreating vehicle and reflected on the one-sided conversation. Indeed, Brooks had many stories of the Grant family, and he'd like nothing better than to share them with Len. However, he had not developed the skill of speaking out loud.

Len's father, Pete, had been a mischief-maker. One time, he saw a tray of cookies sitting on the windowsill of a neighbor's kitchen. She had probably put them there to cool. With his trusty slingshot, Pete picked a cherry from a nearby tree, loaded his weapon, and aimed it at the open window. The cherry went flying. The neighbor lady ran out the back door to see where the missile had come from. At the same time, Pete went to the window, grabbed a handful of cookies, and took off. He ran into the woods to enjoy his loot and didn't think the woman knew who had done it. However, later in the afternoon, she was at Brooks' doorway and told his mother all the details.

Another time, there was a balloon festival in town, and Pete decided to participate. He swiped a bunch of balloons, blew them up, and attached them to every tree, lamppost, and mailbox in town. Again, he thought he got away with his mischief, until someone showed up on Brooks' doorstep to tattle. He had to spend time cleaning up the riot of color as a punishment.

There were many more such tales.

Brooks thought about that big old cave on the adjoining property with an entry on Brooks' fence line. Rumor mills kept alive aged stories of ghostly growls coming from deep within. Those tales were mainly told at night by campers whose faces appeared luminous with firelight and whose eyes darted at their surroundings to keep watch. The tales were meant to keep children from misbehaving, and that's not nice.

Then, there was Old Mrs. Sugar Maple and her mailbox. She was so protective of that little mailbox. She had been planted as a twig many years before Brooks became a house. She proudly sent her helicopter seedlings yearly to prove she was still alive and productive. She brought more attention to herself in the fall when her leaves changed color. Brooks had always tried to stay one step ahead of the fussy old tree. She seemed to think that her seniority allowed her special consideration.

She insisted the mailbox be hidden, and the years of overgrowth accommodated that decision with tree-sized shrubs keeping it out of sight. The overgrown bark-laden sappy tree was like a thorn in Brooks' backyard. It was a downright mischief-maker, and since it was so close to the outside world, it got away with being bold and blatantly rude.

Len pulled into the driveway of his family home. He sat a few moments behind the wheel, thinking about the day's happenings, and he looked forward to a quiet evening at home and an early bedtime. Just as he unbuckled his seat belt, he felt a rapid fluttering in his throat radiating down his neck and into his left arm. A feeling of discomfort settled in his shoulder, but it wasn't painful and was over almost as quickly as it had started. He massaged his neck and then his left shoulder.

"That was weird," he said.

He opened the truck door and stepped out but had to brace himself as a wave of dizziness passed through his body. He shook his head, took a few deep breaths, and then started to walk. When he got to the front door, he stopped, took a couple more deep breaths, and went inside. He was happy to see his wife's familiar face.

"Welcome home, dear. I haven't heard from you all day and missed you."

Dora accepted the silent invitation when he put his arms around her.

"Hey, you look pale. Are you okay?"

"I'm just tired, hon. I've had a full day and am glad to be home. I'm looking forward to a quiet evening while holding hands with my best girl and watching television. I'll probably turn in early."

"Are you sure you're okay?"

"Yeah, I'm fine, stop fussing over me."

They mutually released the embrace.

"Okay. I hope you're interested in a good meal to round off your day because I've been busy in the kitchen. Get washed up, and then come back and keep me company while I finish some things. You can catch me up on what's been keeping you occupied today."

Len kissed her cheek and went to their bedroom to freshen up for dinner. He took the poem he had written out of his pocket and tossed it in the nightstand drawer at his bedside. He went to the bathroom, splashed cold water on his face, and scrubbed his hands while studying his reflection in the mirror. He dried his hands and once more tried to shrug off the tightness in his left shoulder.

"Shake it off, old boy, just shake it off," he advised the man staring back at him in the mirror. He went back to the kitchen and sat on a barstool at the counter.

"You look better. You're sure everything's okay?" asked Dora.

Len smiled. "It's getting there, Dora. It's going to be wonderful. We, my beautiful wife, are going to be innkeepers."

"Len, thanks for working so hard to make this happen. I know you must be exhausted."

"I'm tired, but I've had a good day. I got a lot of work done, too, and with Roger coming this weekend to finish the projects I gave him, we'll be ready to stock the place. How are your plans coming for the open house?"

Dora stood behind him and wiped her hands on her apron. She wrapped her arms around his chest and rested her head on his back. She closed her eyes and squeezed him gently.

"Ann will help me with that this weekend while you and Roger work. Plan on taking the twins with you and putting them to work. I won't have them laying around here all day playing games on their phones."

Dora released her hold on Len and returned to the counter to continue her preparations.

"Dinner is in the oven. Why don't you take a short nap. I'll wake you in an hour."

Len relaxed in his favorite chair, closed his eyes, and daydreamed. He smiled as he visualized his plan taking shape. He would throw a party to celebrate the anniversary of their engagement. They didn't usually commemorate that anniversary, but Len wanted to do something special for his best girl this year. Maybe it could be a part of Brooks' grand opening. He would wrap the deed to Brooks in fancy paper and include a copy of their *net worth* statement. He would put it all together and cover it with a big red bow.

He would present it to his lady and tell her how it came to be. The big finish would be the monogrammed necklace. The monogram BG was initially made for his great-grandmother, Beth Grant, but now it would be BG for Best Girl. He would clasp it around her neck while reciting the poem he had penned. With that, he slipped into slumber.

"Len, dinner is ready."

Len awoke to Dora standing over him. He sat up, stretched, went to the table, and happily watched her present one of his favorite meals—shepherd pie, a tossed salad with ranch dressing, and homemade yeast rolls.

"This looks good. Dora, would you say grace?"

Dora smiled. "Absolutely, Heavenly Father, please bless this food. We are thankful for it, as well as all of our blessings. We ask for thy blessings to help us recognize need, and to be your hands in helping others where we can. Please watch over us and our family. In Jesus' name, Amen."

She looked up. "I made a peach cobbler, too, and I'll put a scoop of that vanilla bean ice cream you like on it."

"I am a lucky man. That little siesta was just what I needed to be fully awake to enjoy this food."

They ate dinner and talked about the history wall they wanted to create at Brooks. They made a list of things they needed to accumulate. After cleaning up, they watched an old movie, the day's news, and the weather report.

Len stood. "I'm going to lock up and shower before turning in. Are you coming to bed?"

"I think I'll read for a little while. I'm tired, too, so reading will likely do me in. I'll be in soon."

"Okay, don't stay up too late. You don't need any beauty sleep, but it never hurts."

Len winked, kissed her cheek, and walked down the hall.

10

*Let go of what you can't change, like rain
on a tin roof— it'll pass.*

"Ms. Davis, I'm ready to leave. The contract for Mr. Grant is in this file. Mark it for signatures and initials and get it to him today. He probably needs a few days to review it but let him know to notify you when it's ready, then pick it up and fax it to the clearing house. Remember to put a copy of the signed contract in the file. They'll get things going on it, and I'll finish it up when I return. Do you have any questions?"

"No, Jake, for the tenth time, I'm fine. I know how to answer phones and make appointments. I don't understand why you have me here for the next three weeks. Except for being a delivery service for this contract, you could have a phone answering service do what you're paying me to do."

Penny finished her blubbering with a pout.

"We've been through this, Penny. I want a physical presence in the office. Use this time to go through old files and organize them like those you've already done. You did a good job. You're smart. Look around and do what needs to be done. Also, don't forget that I told you if you complete a few of the free paralegal courses online, I will consider helping you get a certificate. This would be an ideal time to get started with that. Do you want to be a certified paralegal?"

"Yes," Penny grumbled.

"The next three weeks will give you a chance to prove that. When I return, let's continue this conversation by reviewing your progress with the paralegal courses. Is it a deal?"

"I guess."

Jake said patiently, "Look, Penny, I need to leave. Sarah and I both love you. I hope you know that. We want to help you succeed. I appreciate knowing you're staying here and handling things while I'm gone. My business means a lot to Sarah, our family, and me. I depend on you to care for it, particularly this Grant matter. Can I count on you?"

Penny didn't say anything.

Karvelas walked over to her and put a comforting hand on her slumped shoulder. "I've got a car service scheduled to pick us up, and I still have things to do. We'll be in touch."

Jake walked away, but when the elevator door closed, Penny counted to five then slammed her hand on her desk. She picked up her nameplate and, with a harrumph in her voice, said, "Penelope A. Davis, Paralegal."

She thudded it back on the desktop, picked up the Grant file, and removed the contract. With sad resolution, she added the sticky notes as instructed. The package ended up in an interoffice memo envelope and then into her impressive leather briefcase. She decided to wait until the following day to contact Grant.

Tonight, she would treat herself to an evening at the spa and then get takeout to enjoy in front of the big-screen television on the main floor of her sister and brother-in-law's house, since no one else would be at home.

When Jake married Sarah, they were automatically saddled with the reigns of being parents to Penelope, Sarah's thirteen-year-old sister. The girl's parents were self-involved narcissists and wanted to be empty nesters as soon as possible. It had been a difficult adjustment for the trio, but Penny managed to get through high school without many problems.

However, since then, it has been one thing after another. She didn't want to attend college and thought getting married could solve her problems. That unfortunate decision hooked her up with a guy who had yet to grow up and was more of an angry dictator than a loving companion. A series of failed relationships followed. And when she finally realized she needed to care for herself, she tried one *get rich quick* scheme after another.

Jake and Sarah worked through college, followed by the rigors of starting a family while Jake built his practice. Penny had called her sister just six months ago to tell her she was in trouble and asked for help. Sarah and Jake rescued her again and brought her back into their lives to help her regain stability.

Dora's day began as usual. She donned her favorite walking attire, strapped on her fanny pack that held her phone, placed her porch cap on over quickly combed hair, and headed out the door. She enjoyed a brisk walk in the neighborhood in the clear morning air. The sun just peeked over the mountains to the east. She loved the quietness of the world, disturbed only by a few barking dogs and the faint crow of a rooster. The reggae played through her headphones enlivening her steps.

When she got back home, she expected to find Len up and getting ready for the day, but the house was tranquil. Generally, Len would have his western music blaring loud enough to be heard throughout the house by this time.

She headed to the bedroom. He was still under the covers. He didn't have to be anywhere, so she decided to let him sleep another hour. It wouldn't hurt for him to catch a few extra winks while she showered and dressed.

She took her time enjoying the hot water and then prepared for the day.

Dora walked over to the bed and touched his shoulder, but he didn't move. She put her hand on his chest, held her breath, and bent down to peer into his face.

"Len, wake up."

But he was much too quiet.

She laid her ear on his chest and stroked his face, hoping he would open his eyes and ask her, "What the hell are you doing?"

Nothing happened. His eyes didn't open, his chest didn't rise, and he didn't flinch when she fanned her fingers through his hair.

Dora stood abruptly.

She stared at his lifeless face, then suddenly wrapped her arms around her chest, and an agonizing moan engulfed her.

"Oh, Len, no! Please don't do this. I need you! Please don't do this."

She leaned over him again and shook his shoulders. "Len! Wake up!"

Shaking, she grabbed her phone and dialed 911.

"911, what is your emergency?"

Dora choked on the words as sobs clutched her throat, "This is…this is Dora Grant. I think my husband is dead. I just found him, and he's…"

"Ms. Grant, are you still there? Ms. Grant, take a deep breath and tell me what happened."

Dora took a massive gulp of air. "I think…I think my husband is dead. Please send someone right away, I don't know what to do."

Still clutching the phone to her ear, Dora fell to her knees and threw herself across Len's chest. Wrenching sobs wracked her body, and her heart felt like it would burst.

"Ma'am, I'm sorry ma'am, can you answer a few questions for me? Could you confirm your address? I've already dispatched a crew to help you. You said your name is Dora, right?"

"Yes, that's me," Dora moaned, wiping her eyes with her hands. "It's 7911 Morton Street."

"Okay, Dora, is your house unlocked. My crew is very close. They're asking if they can go in when they arrive."

"Yes, the door is unlocked. I think I hear sirens."

"Great, they're not far from you. Now, Dora, are you certain he's dead?"

"He isn't responding to my touch or my voice, and yes," she sobbed. "His body is cold."

"Has your husband been sick or complained about not feeling well?"

"No, he's been busy with an old house we inherited. I've worried he's doing too much, but what will I do now?"

Dora wailed another agonizing cry.

"He came home last night and said he was tired and wanted to go to bed a little early… Oh, I see the ambulance is pulling up now."

"Please stay on the phone until they are inside and have taken over. You can release me once they are there. I'm so sorry, Mrs. Grant."

Dora heard a clamor of people entering her home and called out to them.

"I'm back here…"

She hadn't finished her response before seeing the faces of four men, all dressed in dark blue uniforms with medical symbols on their pocket flaps. Two of the men carried a portable stretcher with wheels and immediately set it on the floor.

"Excuse me, ma'am, are you Mrs. Grant?"

"Yes, I think my husband is gone," she whispered as though a murmur would make it less so. She heard the 911 operator through the phone, "Mrs. Grant, I can hear them. I'm going to hang up now."

Dora nodded.

An EMT touched her arm. "I'm sorry, Mrs. Grant, let us take a look. Could you give us some room here?"

The worker with a name tag identifying him as Polk gently guided her away from the bed. Dora looked down at Len and allowed herself to be steered to the doorway, her mind spinning with unanswered questions. She watched the commotion and slowly backed out of the room and into the hall—the gravity of what was happening created an invisible heaviness weighing her shoulders. Dora staggered to the living room in defeat and dropped into a chair, holding her head in both hands. Within minutes, she felt a gentle touch and looked up with tear-filled eyes into Polk's compassionate face.

"Mrs. Grant, I'm sorry to confirm your husband has passed. It's hard to tell what might have caused this. My team will move Mr. Grant, and someone from the coroner's office will be in touch later today to update you."

Dora nodded.

"We don't want to leave you alone, so my partner and I will stay behind until we're sure you're okay. Do you have family nearby or a friend or a neighbor who can come over and be with you?"

Dora stared into space. "My family all live many miles away."

"What about a neighbor or a friend," Polk suggested gently.

Dora seemed to regain some composure momentarily and nodded her head.

"Yes, my friend Jean lives nearby. I'll call her."

She realized she still had her phone in a tight grip and dialed Jean's number. The phone rang three times before it was answered.

"Hello," said Jean.

"Jean, it's Dora. I need you to come over. Something happened to Len, and I need you."

Dora nodded as though Jean could see the assenting gesture before hanging up the phone without a parting acknowledgment. She dropped the phone in her lap and breathlessly said, "Thanks, Jean."

Dora looked at the EMT. "She's my friend, she'll be here soon."

"That's good."

The sound of wheels rolling on the tile caused Dora and Polk to turn toward the hall. One of the workers held the litter board as he pulled it while another worker pushed from the foot end. Len's form was covered up to his shoulders with a white sheet.

Dora stood and went to her husband. The workers respectfully made space for her as she bent over his body, kissed his lips, and stroked his face. She ran her fingers through his wavy silver hair.

A tear splashed on the face of the man she adored, and as it splintered, she wiggled her nose and smiled into his unseeing face.

Len was gone.

They covered his head with the sheet and wheeled his body away.

Grief overtook her, and she collapsed into a chair.

No sooner had the ambulance pulled out of the driveway than Jean stormed through the door.

She ran to her friend and threw her arms around Dora.

"Oh, Dora, I'm so sorry. What happened? Was there an accident?"

Jean hugged her gal pal of thirty-plus years. Through tears and with no words, they wept together.

The EMT, named Polk, said, "We're going to go now, Mrs. Grant. I'll leave this card on the table if you need to contact us."

"Thanks, guys," said Jean. "I'll stay with her. I won't leave until one of her family gets here."

The paramedics left.

"Jean, I've got to call the kids. What do I tell them?"

"You tell them that their father has passed away, and they need to come home and help you. This isn't something you can shield your children from, Dora. Can I get you anything?"

Dora shook her head.

"Has he been sick, Dora?"

"No, and it wasn't an accident. He was tired last night, but that's all." Dora looked at Jean. "I think he may have had a heart attack." She put her face in her hands and tears leaked through her fingers.

"Oh, Dora. I'm so sorry." She stood abruptly, went to the kitchen, and returned shortly with two bottles of water.

Dora put her bottle on the floor and stared at it. The two women sat in silence for several minutes.

Dora took a long, labored breath. "I guess I had better call the kids."

"Do you want me to call them?"

"No, I will, thanks." She glanced at her phone but asked, "What time is it anyway?"

"Umm, almost ten."

"Okay, Roger is probably at the store. I've got that number in my phone. I don't know where Hannah is. She's always flying somewhere for work, and Robyn just moved to Australia. I don't even know the time of day right now in Australia. I hate waking them up."

A fresh onslaught of tears caused her to convulse with emotion.

"Little Lenny, he'll never understand this. Len is always so cute with him. I guess I should say, 'he was.'"

"Dora, one thing at a time, you call Roger now. It doesn't matter if he's at the store, call him."

Dora stood, walked across the floor, and sank into the sofa.

"Try Hannah's cell phone," said Jean. "If she doesn't answer the first time, keep trying. Repeated calls should alert her that there's an emergency. I'm going to figure out what time it is in Australia."

Jean joined her friend on the sofa, smiled at her, and gave her a reassuring squeeze as she pulled out her phone.

Penny placed a call to Len Grant. The phone rang a half-dozen times before an invitation to leave a message came on. She hung up and made a note to herself to call later.

Sarah had a lot of houseplants and had left specific instructions about the schedule she wanted kept in their upkeep, so Penny tended to them. She wandered around the house, peeked in drawers, and snooped in closets. She watched a few of the morning shows on television. Then did a somewhat sloppy google search about paralegal certification before getting lost on the web again researching bearer bonds.

Ms. Penelope got to the office mid-morning. She was greeted with a ringing phone and noted the flashing light on the answering machine. None of the calls were urgent, and she managed to get through them by noon. During her break, she tried Len Grant's cell phone again.

No answer.

She spent the better part of the afternoon knee-deep in old files. Her last official act of the day was to call Len Grant, but there was still no answer.

11

Remember, you're as sturdy as a cedar tree;
Stand tall and proud.

Dora awoke slowly, and her eyes gradually focused on daylight, barely making itself known between the shutters of her bedroom. For the second morning in a row, she became aware of her new reality, a life without Len, and again asked, how could this happen?

This time last week, they were both full of life planning and dreaming and idealizing like they were young married again. Her grief felt heavy, flattening her deeper into the mattress, stifling her with its weight. How can life change so quickly? How can a man's heart, soul, and breath be reversed so instantaneously?

She rolled into her pillow and cried. "How will I ever live without him," she said.

In the last forty-eight hours, she asked herself these questions in hundreds of different ways without a suitable answer, not even an unsuitable one. She closed her eyes and pictured Len, his smile, the wavy hair, glistening blue eyes, the mustache, and the comforting warmth of his arms. She tried to hear his voice, but instead, her thoughts were interrupted by a rap on her door.

That's right, she wasn't alone.

Roger and his family arrived within hours of being notified. Hannah got in early yesterday morning, and with the arrival of Robyn and her family last night, the house was packed.

The door hinges accompanied a small whisper, "Grammy."

Dora kept her eyes closed but had no problem picturing two little girls tiptoeing to her bedside. She could feel them studying her and then heard a quiet voice.

"Be quiet. She might still be asleep. Remember, Mama said we should be quiet. Grammy is very tired, Mama said, and she needs to sleep. Let's watch her until she wakes up."

"I am quiet, Rachel. Don't be bossy. I'm being quiet, just like you. I'm big, just like you, and I know how to be quiet. I'm not a baby. Lenny's a baby, not me."

Dora kept her eyes closed, enjoying her granddaughters' voices, and trying very hard to maintain a neutral look on her sleepy face. Her heart softened with this reminder of the goodness within her arms grasp.

Oh, how Len loved his grandchildren and couldn't get enough of the energy they exuded. That is where his love for nature extended to human nature. He even named some of his special roses after his granddaughters, and they took delight in knowing they had namesakes. They visited the pretty yellow roses named Rachel and the barely pink roses named Elizabeth. No one was allowed to call the pink rose by anything other than Elizabeth because, according to Grandpa, they deserved a regal, beautiful name. After that, little Lizzie reminded people that her actual name was Elizabeth because she, too, was regal. One of her big boy cousins asked her what she thought regal meant, and she told the boy, "I don't know, but it sounds nice."

Dora couldn't stay quiet much longer. The grief in her heart would have to find a temporary abode while she enjoyed the life within her grasp at this very minute. So, she quickly opened both eyes and exclaimed just above a whisper, "Boo."

The girls shrieked in delight as Dora sat up and hung her legs off the side of the bed. She held out her arms, and both girls joyfully took the invitation, wrapping themselves around her neck. She fell backward onto the bed with sugar, spice, and everything nice tucked under each arm, cuddling with all her might.

"Did you girls sleep well? Do you like the bunkbeds Grampy made for you?"

"I didn't have any bad dreams, Grammy. I like to dream about unicorns and rainbows. Have you ever seen a unicorn, Grammy? I wanted to see a real unicorn, but Daddy said he couldn't find one," the words tumbled out of Lizzie's mouth. She closed her eyes. "I can see a unicorn right now."

Rachel leaned into Dora's ear and whispered, "Mommy said it's okay for Lizzie to see unicorns cause she's still little. I used to see unicorns when I was little, too. Did you ever see unicorns, Grammy?"

The whole unicorn conversation ended with the inclusion of "snips and snails and puppy dog tails" in the joyful prattle and running feet of Grandpa Len's namesake. Dora and the girls sat up and focused on the energetic two-year-old doing his best to join the crowd.

He grabbed the comforter with both hands while his feet clamored to find the leverage to hoist himself up. After a few failed attempts, the older two girls got a firm grip on the backside of his pajamas and helped him finish the ascent.

Lenny immediately stood and started to jump on the bed, giggling with every bounce. He enjoyed the makeshift trampoline for a bit before Dora caught little Len midflight and set him on her lap between his sisters.

The little boy's mood suddenly darkened as he took in the room, settling his eyes on the empty side of the bed and a pillow that had not been flattened. He asked the inevitable question.

"Where's Grumpy?"

"Lenny, you're not supposed to ask Grammy that question. Did you forget what Mama said?"

"It's okay, Rachel," assured Dora, who studied the inquisitive expression on the boy's face and the look of grown-up concern on his sisters' faces.

"Tell me what your Mama told you about where Grampy is."

"You tell her, Rachel, I get mixed up," said Liz.

"She said Grampy is old, so his soul left his body."

Lizzie suddenly recollected the conversation and quickly added, "And she said that someday we will see him again when our souls leave our bodies, but that won't happen for a long time because we're young."

She then looked at her grandmother with all the intensity of sweet innocence. "Grammy, are you old? Will your soul leave your body soon?"

Dora smiled at the guilelessness surrounding her. An old quote came to mind, "*we must put away all effort to impress and come with the guileless candor of childhood.*" She wanted to be honest with these children but didn't want to scare them with too much reality. She said a silent prayer to be able to vocalize an appropriate response.

"I am getting old, but no one knows when their soul might leave their body. We must take excellent care of our bodies, be kind to one another, and try to make the world a better place every day we are here. We'll all miss Grampy, and I'll bet he misses us. Whenever you want to talk to your Grampy, close your eyes, think of him, and talk to him if you want to. That's what I do."

"Like I do when I want to see a unicorn?" asked Lizzie.

"Yes, sweetheart, like you do when you want to see a unicorn."

Another rap on the door announced the arrival of Dora's youngest child. The mother of the three youngsters all piled around their grandmother.

"You little monkeys, what are you doing in here?" said Robyn. "I told you we wanted to let Grammy sleep, and you're in here making noise. I'm sorry, Mom, I've been organizing the kitchen. You've so much food that's been dropped off, and I thought these little darlings were watching cartoons downstairs."

Robyn bent down and gently mussed the hair of three little heads. They responded with giggles, trying to wriggle away from her.

"Oh, they're fine. I was feeling a little down, and they cheered me up."

Dora tickled each child under the chin. Rachel squirmed away from her grandmother and reminded her siblings of the morning television lineup.

"Lizzie, Lenny, let's go find Paw Patrol on TV."

The girls jumped off the bed and tore down the hall, racing downstairs. Lenny inched himself off the bed feet first and did his best to keep up with his sisters while shouting, "Ryder, Ryder."

The quiet room begged for conversation.

"How are you feeling this morning, Mom? What would you like for breakfast?"

"Thanks, Robyn. Give me some time to get cleaned up and dressed. I don't want anything heavy. Maybe a yogurt or a piece of fruit. What about all of you? Have you eaten?"

"Don't worry about us. The kids had cereal, and the rest of us did the continental breakfast thing. We're big enough to take care of ourselves, Mom. We're here to help you. Roger made an appointment to go to the mortuary tomorrow and scheduled the church for the services. He, Ann, and the boys are at Brooks today to look around. Brian said he was tagging along to help Roger with some projects Dad lined up. There were some things Roger and Dad started a week ago, and they intended to finish them today."

"That will be nice, I know that would make Dad happy."

Robyn continued her report on the family's plans. "Hannah and I are staying here with the kids, although I might pay a visit or two to a couple of friends to give you a break from the noise of my little monsters. Hannah plans on staying put all day. Do you have any errands you want me to run?"

"I can't think of anything dear." She furrowed her brow. "And those little angels are not monsters."

"I know, I'm lucky to have them. I can't imagine being fulfilled without them. However, I have to admit they drive me crazy sometimes."

"I'll tell you from experience that 'craziness' is entirely reversible, and you'll long for it in days to come. It's over much too soon, and I say that with all the wisdom of old age."

Dora's older daughter, Hannah, was just coming in as Robyn was leaving.

"Hi, sis," said Robyn when she passed her. "How's it going today?"

"It's going good. I just wanted to see how Mother is."

Dora called to Robyn, "You won't be going before I finish getting ready, will you?"

"No, Mom, I haven't even started preparing the kids for the day. I'll need to pry them away from Paw Patrol, and I know from experience that won't be easy," said Robyn.

Dora asked, "Are you coming in, Hannah?"

Hannah walked into the room. "Mother, I'm right here. I've been up for hours. I had a virtual meeting this morning, so I've been in Dad's office on my laptop."

Dora looked at her daughter. "Are you okay, Hannah?"

"I'm fine, Mom. The question is, how are you?"

"Oh, sweetheart, I'm as fine as possible. It's just hard wrapping my head around all of this. If your dad had been sick, I may have had some time to be prepared. I knew we weren't getting any younger, but I thought we'd have another twenty years together. He's been working so hard on Brooks, and I begged him repeatedly to slow down. We didn't even get a golden wedding anniversary. I've always assumed we'd have that."

Hannah bristled. "I wish you and Dad would have sold Brooks, Mom."

"Well, we didn't," said Dora.

"I know, Mother, I'm sorry. You and Daddy have been wonderful examples to all of us about commitment. Life gets complicated. I'm confident you'll be okay."

Dora looked at her daughter and sensed there was something more she wanted to say. She knew of Hannah's objection to the bed-and-breakfast project. That had been the subject of more than one conversation, and Dora hoped it wouldn't be an inevitable subject of contention, especially now. She steeled herself as Hannah started to speak.

"Honestly, Mother, when we all gathered in the family room after Robyn, Brian, and the kids arrived last night, it was so much fun. It reminded me of the days when we kids were teenagers, and you guys worked so hard to get us to enjoy family nights around the game table. I'm afraid we weren't all that cooperative most of the time. Last night, I longed for those days when life was so simple. Since I graduated from college ten years ago and immediately took on this job, I've always been off to a meeting, trying to unravel some complexity in the business or working to soothe somebody's inflated ego or unruffle someone's sensitive feathers. Reliving old memories last night was relaxing and would have been perfect had Daddy been here."

Dora teared up.

"Oh, Mother, I'm so sorry. That was a selfish thing for me to say. Please forgive me."

"Nonsense, sweetheart, we're all hurting. It's okay, we'll get through this. None of us could do it alone, we're blessed to have each other. Are you aware, my sweet child, how proud your dad and I are of you?"

"Of me, what did I do?"

"You are a very successful young woman, taking care of yourself in a competitive business. I marvel at your sense of confidence. You're well-educated, poised, and on the road to becoming a top-level executive in an impressive industry. Your dad and I brag about you all the time."

"Thanks, but you know I look at Roger and Ann with their business and their boys and then at Robyn and Brian and their beautiful little family living worldwide and being exposed to diverse cultures. Sometimes, I feel like I'm missing out."

"Hannah, there's still time for you to have all that. If you want a family, start looking for opportunities to enjoy that part of life. Don't give up. You're beautiful, smart, accomplished, and well-educated. Decide what you need to complete your life if you feel unfulfilled, and make it happen."

"Thanks for your encouragement. I'll consider it between my business meetings and reports, which were all due yesterday. In the meantime, I have a few calls to make, so I better get back to work. Love you, Mother."

"Love you, too, my darling."

12

Mistakes are lessons learned, like plowing a crooked row.

Penny tried Len's phone yet again, getting the same frustrating result, only now it went straight to voice mail. She knew she needed to get the contract to him, and Jake had told her not to involve the Grant family. She drove to the Brooks house, hoping to run into him there. Penny had gone past the old house many times and wondered about it. As a kid, she had heard rumors about it being haunted.

Brooks came into view as she drove around the curved driveway, and she had to admit she was impressed with its curb appeal. She parked in front of the house and approached the front door with her fancy briefcase in hand. She noticed a brand-new doormat with a calligraphy greeting, "Welcome to Brooks — Come on In." It had a flourish beneath the writing.

"You'd think they could do better than that ugly thing," she said. She stepped on it, and it seemed to shift, throwing her a little off balance.

"Whoa, what was that?"

She lifted her shoe to see if she had broken a heel or stepped on a rock, but everything appeared normal.

When she pressed the doorbell, she felt a little "zing" radiate up her arm.

"Stupid doorbell," she stammered as she hammered on the doorframe with her fist tightly clenched.

Penelope Davis couldn't have known that the doorbell and the doormat were long-term friends—one always had the other's back.

The door opened, revealing an ashen-haired woman wearing baggy jeans and an oversized T-shirt. Her hair was pulled back from her face and piled in a messy bun. Her casual clothing and athletic figure were paired with a sullen expression and somber tone.

"Yes, what can I do for you?"

"I'm Penelope Davis. I'm with the Karvelas Law Firm and need to see Mr. Grant. Is he here?"

Ann Grant pondered how much information she should give strangers at this point. She decided to find her husband, Roger Grant, and let him decide. She opened the door further and stepped to one side, beckoning the stranger into the house.

"I'm Mr. Grant's daughter-in-law. My husband is out back in the garden. Come in, and I'll get him. It may take a few minutes. The library is through that door. You can get comfortable there if you like."

Ann left through the back door, and Penny slowly turned, eyeing Brooks' entryway. She strolled into the library and spied a massive desk against a backdrop of shelves filled with books. Penny put her briefcase on the desk, opened it, and took out the contract envelope. She assumed Len Grant was with his son, and she wanted to get the contract signed and get out of this place. It felt creepy to her.

"I'd turn this room into a game room with a pool table, ping pong, and snack machines to bring in revenue." She talked to herself, but it was loud enough to be heard by someone or *something.*

The air conditioner grumbled.

At first, it startled Penny, and she jumped, berating herself for being high-strung.

The air conditioner's hum settled into a pattern.

She thought she heard, "Not nice, not nice, not nice, not nice."

Penny looked around, sure there must be someone in the room messing with her.

The sound continued. Then, it stopped as suddenly as it began, and Ms. Penny let out a weak laugh. Her façade of confidence seemed to be slipping away like the ocean's ebb at low tide.

"Settle down, Penny. Don't let this decrepit place get under your skin."

Penny studied the booklined shelves and realized that this library was filled with many genres, leather-bound books were abundant.

"Wow, leather-bound books. Grant ought to 'sell' some of these. I'll bet there are collectors out there willing to pay a pretty penny for them."

She loved using the expression "pretty penny" to compliment herself.

She reached for one of the fancy books, but it seemed stuck. It wouldn't move but an inch from the shelf. She tried with both hands, assuming the book was wedged somehow. Suddenly it pulled free, and she tumbled to the floor. The book bonked her on the head and landed on the floor next to her.

Penny shook her head. She got up from the floor, picked up the book, and placed it on the desk.

She felt something buzz and a shiver ran down her spine. She glanced over her shoulder expecting to see someone. The buzzing continued, and she realized it was her phone. She dug it out of her pocket and touched the answer icon.

"This is Ms. Davis."

"Penny, it's Jake. Did you get that document signed yet?"

"Jake, where are you? You sound like you're underwater."

"I assure you that I'm not underwater, but this connection is awful. I asked you a question. Did you get that document signed?"

"No, I'm at the Brooks house now. I tried calling Mr. Grant repeatedly, but it just went to voice mail. I decided to come out here and find him. The woman answering the door asked me to wait in the library for him."

"Penny, if that's his wife, please don't tell her…, Len …a surprise…," said Jake.

"It wasn't his wife. She was a daughter or something. Don't worry, I'll take care of it."

Penny was unnerved, and the added exasperation in dealing with her boss didn't help. He seemed to always make her feel so inadequate.

"Penny, can you hear me? I'm inside now. Penny, Penny, are you still there?"

"I can hear you. Stop yelling."

"The cell service here is terrible, and where I'm headed is even worse. I should have activated global roaming on my phone before I left. I'm looking for a shop here where I can pick up a local SIM card. I'll get back to you as soon as I do that. Please let me know as soon as you've got that document signed and remember to fax it to the contact info I left for you. It's all in the Grant file. I can't stress enough how important this is."

"I will, Jake. I remember every…"

The line buzzed, and she knew she had lost the call. She turned at the sound of someone entering the room.

"Hello, Ms. Davis, I'm Roger, Len Grant's son. What can I do for you?

Penny turned to see a younger version of the man she met in the law office several days ago.

"I'm Penelope Davis. I'm here to deliver a document to Len Grant. Is he on the property somewhere?"

Roger glanced at the woman before he turned to the open briefcase on the desk.

"No, I'm sorry, my father isn't here."

Roger braced himself. It was still hard to talk about his father's passing without choking up.

"He died four days ago. We don't know for sure, but we think he may have had a heart attack. I don't want to bother my mother with business decisions. Can you tell me what this is all about?"

"First of all, Mr. Grant, my condolences about your father. It's a business matter regarding the probate our firm is handling for Mr. Grant," she lied. "This can wait. It's just a few loose threads we want to trim. I'll give your mother some time and contact her later."

"I'd rather you wait for maybe a week or even two?"

Penny nodded. "Of course, you're right."

"Thanks, Ms. Davis. My wife and I own the hardware store in Leming, a few hours north of here. I'll add my mother's number to the back of my card." Roger pulled out one of his business cards from his wallet, jotted down his mother's number on the back, and handed it to Penny. "Don't hesitate to call me if there's anything I can do to help my mother."

"Yes, I'll do that. I don't know how this will be affected by your father's untimely death, but we'll make sure it's taken care of. Again, I'm very sorry. I met him several times, and he seemed like a wonderful man."

Roger smiled at the woman and nodded. "He was, we're all going to miss him."

Penny picked up the envelope but dropped it like a hot potato. It gave off an electric jolt and seemed to wrestle from her grip. She looked at her fingers, expecting to see them scorched, then softly grazed the pads of her four fingers against her thumb. She grabbed the wrinkled edges of the envelope, stuffed it back in the leather case, and picked up her bag by the handle.

It dangled precariously.

"That's weird." She stared at the detached handle. "This bag is almost new."

Roger didn't say anything.

Penny clutched the bag with both hands, held it to her chest, and preceded Roger out the library door. Surprisingly, the front door was wide open. Maybe it was her imagination, but it seemed to quiver as she approached it. She crossed the threshold, purposely avoiding the doormat, and pressed the button on her car key fob.

The door lock didn't release on the first, second, or third try, but the fourth time the lock popped up. She opened the car door, tossed her briefcase onto the passenger seat, and plopped behind the wheel. Penny pulled the door closed, took a deep breath, and closed her eyes. She leaned forward and put her face in her hands.

She felt like someone was looking at her, and she looked up into Roger Grant's concerned face.

She fumbled but realized she needed to turn the key on. Penny put the key into the ignition, turned it, and opened the window.

"Are you okay, Ms. Davis? Do you need some water or something?"

Penny shook her head and managed a weak wave as she pulled away from the creepy old house, steering her way down the driveway.

As far as she was concerned, the house was a bunch of rotted old lumber, rusty pipes, and shorted wiring. Yet Len Grant had described it as a piece of heaven set in the Garden of Eden.

Things started to come together in Penny's mind. Len Grant had died, and his widow didn't know about the bearer bonds. Perhaps she didn't even realize she had possession of them.

"If this were my place, I'd turn the whole thing into a complex of high-rise apartments," she said.

Her car sputtered and ground to a halt under the bent limbs of a maple tree just as she neared the exit to the road. Sap dripped onto the windshield of the driver's side of the car.

"What is that?"

She traced the glutinous substance trailing down her windshield with her finger. She grabbed some pre-moistened tissues from the seat, got out, and wiped the sap away. She looked up to see where it had come from, just in time for a glob of the sticky goo to smack her in the face.

She wiped away the gunk, got back in, and started the car. Thankfully, it purred.

She cussed the house, the grounds, and the overgrown sugar maple tree, and pulled onto the main road.

During the drive home, she sputtered about Brooks, and without much trouble, created a plan to possess the bearer bonds. Jake wouldn't return for another two and a half weeks so Penny would wait a respectable week to contact Dora Grant and then spin a story about how the bonds were useless, but that the company would reward her with a few thousand dollars in exchange for the bonds to get them out of circulation.

Once Penny had possession of the bonds, she would bid farewell to this place and everything about it. Thankfully, her passport was up to date. Six months from now, she pictured herself on a beach wearing a new bikini, soaking up the sun's rays, and reading a trashy novel. Her daydream also included listening to her favorite Spotify list and being sought after by a hot-looking lifeguard. An added benefit would be never having to be subject to the hoity-toity ways of the Karvelas family again.

Brooks watched as the woman approached his door and entered his domicile. It didn't take long for him to peg her as being self-absorbed. He had known many like her. Some had only visited, and some had lived within his walls. He remembered Old Mrs. Sugar Maple referring to people like that as Grumpy Pants People.

He wasn't exactly happy about how the doormat and doorbell treated the visitor. He advocated being nice to everyone. However, he knew the pair to be close. He would talk with them later about the importance of first impressions.

Later, he found out about what happened in the library and the shenanigans of old Mrs. Maple. It was getting harder and harder to oversee this group, and he coughed up a lint ball stuck in his furnace filter.

Brooks sensed the spirit of Len entering his walls and recalled the long-ago days when the carefree little boy ran the halls. Now, the house and the soul of the man called Len spent time in solitude, often appreciating that the most authentic connection lies not in the words we speak but in the silent moments we share. And that the most meaningful conversations are the ones where there are no words at all.

Len's untimely death had surprised Brooks, who certainly didn't have the power to overrule those things. He deferred to the Great One and knew there must be a purpose in it.

When Penelope Davis left the premises, Brooks' rafters and floors released merry creaks, his window casements hugged shining panes, prisms glimmered suspended from chandeliers, drapes perfectly framed the outdoor views, and an invisible goodness returned to the house. The doorbell wires securely attached, and the doormat settled nicely so as not to trip guests.

A fresh evening breeze whispered through the leaves of the old sugar maple tree.

"Nicely done." The hulking mass of timber accepted the compliment with branches stretching high in the sky as she watched Ms. Grumpy Pants and her wheeled machine disappear across the horizon.

13

Find joy in life's simple pleasures, like a sunset on the porch.

"Hi, Mom, it's Roger. Sorry, we're running late, but we're stopping for takeout, so don't fix anything. The boys have suggested pizza, do you have any special requests?"

"No, dear, anything you choose is fine. But we have a lot of food here, we can warm up something. Grandma Eva and her friend Abe will be here, too. She wants to be with the family tonight since it's the eve before the funeral."

"Oh, that's great, should we stop and pick her up? We have plenty of room for her and Abe."

"She called about fifteen minutes ago and expected her Uber any minute."

"Do you think pizza is okay for them?"

"Oh, sure. Besides, we have other choices if not."

"This place has a great salad bar. I'll get a family-sized salad, too. Brian wants to know whether Robyn has returned from her forays around town?"

"No, but she just called, she'll be here in half an hour. It's just Hannah and me."

"Okay, we'll be there by then."

"What has kept you so busy at Brooks today?"

"Dad wanted that area by the old sugar maple tree cleaned out so people could see oncoming traffic better. It was like pulling teeth to get all the underbrush cleaned out. But it looks great now, and it'll be much safer. Devon and Luke were a big help with their young muscles."

"That will make him happy."

"You'll never guess what we found."

"What?"

"We found a mailbox, Mom. It's a miniature version of what Brooks initially looked like. It was a little worn but not bad. Ann put a fresh coat of paint on it, and it looks great now. I'm bringing it home. It needs a key, but if you don't have one, I'll see if I can jimmy it open."

"I haven't seen anything of a spare key, but it might be in that box your dad said he left at the house for me. He said there were a bunch of historical-type things in it. Let's not damage the lock in case it's there."

"Right, bye, Mom. I love you."

"Love you, too."

"It looks like we're having pizza and salad for dinner tonight, Hannah. "

"I haven't had pizza in ages. I purposely stayed away from it for a long time, but these days, I see it as a welcome treat on occasion."

"I always have a few frozen pizzas on hand, and your dad and I would enjoy one interspersed with dinner at Wendy's for our date nights. It's going to be different fixing meals for one."

Dora's eyes clouded as she swallowed the beginning of a sob.

"Mother, what's it like?"

"What are you talking about? Are you asking me to describe grief?"

"No, not at all. What is it like to meet someone and to know that person is the one you want to spend forever with? How do you know when it's right? I have friends and associates worldwide, and I see a lot of apathy among couples. People who thought they had it right only to realize it's all wrong. You and Daddy have been together for decades. I don't remember ever feeling like either of you was disappointed or unhappy with the decision to marry. I wonder, how do you do it?"

"Well, I guess I've never thought about it. First, we married young, so we only had a little time to form preconceived ideas about marriage. We just knew we wanted to be together. We wanted to wake up every morning in the same bed and sleep every night in one another's arms. We didn't analyze anything or worry about what may be ahead. We just assumed we could manage life better as a twosome. And then, as our children came along, we determined that our kids needed us to be a united front. I don't think there was ever a time when we considered trying to go our separate ways."

"You make it sound so simple, but to me, it seems formidable."

"It's funny to hear you voice it that way, Hannah, because your dad often described me as a *formidable woman*, and I never understood what he meant. Perhaps you've been inspired by your dad to explain that word to me."

Dora continued, "Look, my precious girl, try not to worry about it. Try to open yourself up and be approachable. I'm sure there's someone out there looking for a young woman like you, likely trying to figure out all the emotions you've just expressed. He's probably confused and frustrated about his lot in life and hoping to find a helpmate like you. In the meantime, take care of yourself and be happy. It'll happen, and you'll be glad you waited it out."

Hannah smiled. "Okay, thanks, Mother." She stood. "I'm going to get cleaned up for dinner."

Hannah stopped her retreat when the front door opened, and Grandma Eva came in followed closely by Old Abe.

Dora said, "Hi, Mom, Abe. I'm glad to see you both."

Eva went to Dora and standing on her tiptoes enveloped her little girl. "How are you holding up dear?"

"I'm okay, Mom, trying to figure things out I guess."

Eva hugged Dora once more, kissed her on the cheek, and with her arm still around Dora's waist, she said, "I didn't want to stay home tonight, and Abe offered to come with me. I needed some company apart from all those old people."

"Grandma, you know you're as old as they are."

Eva flashed her granddaughter a snarky glance.

Abe approached Dora, took her hand in both of his, and said, "I'm so sorry for your loss Ms. Dora. I know what it's like to lose a partner. You're in my thoughts and prayers."

"Thank you, Abe, I appreciate your kindness."

"Hope you don't mind me tagging along," said Abe. "I didn't want my girl here riding those Uber things unaccompanied, you know."

Abe had to be almost ninety years old and seemed to imagine being capable of fighting off bad guys in defense of his ladylove. He was as naughty as he was charming, and his constant good-naturedness was contagious. He made a beeline for Hannah.

"Hannah, I'm always glad to see a vision of loveliness."

The old gentleman presented himself like a knight in armor, took Hannah's hand, and brought it to his lips as he bowed as far as he could manage from the waist.

Hannah laughed like a schoolgirl.

"Abe, you are a charmer. How has Grandma managed to steal you away from all your conquests at home? And Grandma, as usual, you look adorable. I'm so glad you came over. We're having pizza and salad, courtesy of Roger and Ann."

Hannah bent to hug her diminutive grandmother. "See you at dinner."

"Dora, why am I not being mobbed by little children?" asked Eva. "Where are they?"

"They'll be here soon. The kids will be excited to see you again. The girls think it's so cool to have a grandma who likes bangles, beads, and glitter as much as they do."

After pizza, the Grant family settled into their evening routine of family stories, and much to the delight of the children, Old Abe regaling them with his boyhood hijinks. Eva had to remind Abe that he was talking with teenage boys who didn't need any bright ideas about mischief-making.

Ann changed the subject. "Roger, did you tell your mother about Ms. Davis?"

"No, I forgot."

"Who's Ms. Davis?" asked Dora.

"I don't know exactly. She wanted to talk to Dad. She said she was from some law office in town. I told her about Dad's passing and suggested she contact you in another week or two. She said she would, so I gave her one of my business cards and your number. Don't worry about it, she said it was something to do with loose ends of the probate and doesn't need to be taken care of immediately."

Dora thought for a minute then she said, "That's odd. Granddad's attorney did all of the probate work."

"Roger, I remember your great-grandpa. He was just a few years older than me. He played a good basketball game," said Abe.

"I didn't know that about him." Suddenly, Roger stood. "Hey, Mom, I just remembered the mailbox. I'm going to get it out of my car. You're gonna love it."

Roger left and returned carrying a cardboard box. He pulled out the likeness of Brooks with a small American flag on a rocker hinge attached to the outside. The children gathered to get a closer look.

"Oh, Roger, this is amazing. How about that? We've got ourselves a miniature version of Brooks. I'm going to display it inside Brooks Bed & Breakfast. I love it."

"I'm glad you like it. It was challenging to get to, though. We intended to cut back the weeds and trim the hedge, but then we saw the mailbox and decided to rescue it. You wouldn't believe how tightly it was wedged into the hedge, and the sugar maple tree is humongous. The trunk has to be at least three feet in diameter, and I swear it must be a hundred feet high. Sometimes, it seemed like there was something underground trying as hard to hold the mailbox down as we were working to get it out."

"Well, I'm glad you were able to get it out. It'll be a great conversation starter."

"Mom, there's one other thing we found. It's pretty worn out, but I didn't have the heart to throw it away without giving you a chance to do something with it. Ann thinks it has promise."

Roger pulled out something wrapped in the shreds of a blanket. He pulled back the rag covering and revealed the saddest-looking doll Dora had ever seen. Roger carefully handed the bundle to his mother, and she delicately stared into the face of the toy. It was dirty, and its clothes were as shredded as the blanket.

"Oh, my goodness. Now, I wonder what her story is?"

It was a rhetorical question, but Roger responded.

"I'm glad that whoever owned her cared enough to tuck her next to the tree trunk. Can you clean her up and use her in your decorating?"

"I hope so. She was special to someone. I'll study her more and see what ideas I can develop. Perhaps I can find a doll hospital and get her admitted, have some professionals look at her."

Roger put the mailbox on the kitchen counter, set the doll back in the box, then said, "Mom, with your permission, I'd like to call a family meeting about tomorrow."

"Of course, dear. Let's gather in the family room."

When the clan claimed their places in chairs or on the floor, Roger clapped his hands and said, "This will be a short meeting about tomorrow, and then we'll play games."

"Okay, I want to ensure we all feel confident about what's happening tomorrow with the funeral. Luke, Devon, do you understand what is expected in being pallbearers?"

Both boys nodded with confidence.

"Rachel and Lizzie, are you ready with the song you're singing?"

The girls nodded.

"Does anyone have any questions at all?"

A tentative little hand raised.

"Yes, Lizzie, what is your question?"

Everyone turned toward the little girl.

"Uncle Roger, is it okay to close my eyes when I sing?"

"Well, sure, that would be okay. You have a pretty voice. If closing your eyes helps, that's fine. Why do you need to close your eyes?"

"It's scary, Uncle Roger, to see all those people. Mama said there would be lots of people, and they would be looking at us while we sang. If I close my eyes, then it won't be scary."

"Okay, then close your eyes. Your mama and Aunt Hannah will be sitting behind you and singing along very softly to help you."

Lizzie looked at her older sister with an *I told you so* expression.

Roger continued, "It's going to be a sad day because we're

going to think of our dad and grandpa, but he would want us to be happy and think about all the times we laughed with him. We need to be at the church by nine, the funeral starts at eleven, followed by a short service at the cemetery.

"Then, we'll come back here to entertain family and friends. A lunch is being provided, but it will be a full day. Take time alone if you need it. I love you all. Is there anything else to say before we start our game night?"

Grandma Eva raised her hand. "This has been fun, but Abe and I should probably go. I need some beauty rest, and you'll notice that Abe has already started his."

Everyone's eyes went to Abe, slumped in a chair, snoring softly.

Eva pulled out her phone. "I'll get an Uber."

"Grandma, I'll take you home. Brian, will you set up the game table?"

Brian nodded. "Okay, Hannah, tonight it's me, you, and Roger against the hooligans. We'll gang up on them and show them how the big kids play. We've got to redeem ourselves from last night's loss. Roger, with your permission, I'd like to issue an order like we do in the Air Force."

"You have my permission, Lieutenant."

Roger saluted his brother-in-law, who summarily returned the sloppy salute and turned on his heel, facing the boys reclined on a couch deeply involved with electronics. Roger ushered his grandmother and her sleepy escort to the car.

"Luke, Devon, I'm talking to you. Put the electronics away. We're playing UNO."

The young teens begrudgingly set the handheld machines aside and eyed one another with conspiratorial grins.

"Okay, you asked for it. Devon and I will clean the house tonight," said Luke.

"I don't know about that," said Hannah. "I feel a lucky streak, and I intend on winning. And tonight, I'm watching you two, so don't pass cards under the table, you little scamps."

"Who, us? I'm offended. What about you, Devon? Are you offended?"

Robyn asked, "Kiddos, you want to choose a game to play with Mama?" She directed her question to the wide-eyed children who happily scampered to the cabinet filled with games.

Ann and Dora lingered on the couch for a while, discussing plans for Brooks' open house before being commanded by the Lieutenant to join the party. Dora headed for the table surrounded by her daughter and the trio of blond heads. "I think I'll play with the little ones," she announced.

"Not me," said Ann, "I need to keep my boys in line."

14

Surround yourself with good-hearted folks;
They'll stick by you like family.

The mailbox sat proudly on the kitchen counter, still basking in the compliments of his appearance. He had been released from the suffocating hold of the old sugar maple tree and was still becoming accustomed to his newfound freedom. He recalled when the daylight blinded him as the brush was cleared. And then the relief he felt upon extraction from the roots of old Mrs. Maple. That was a battle to the last minute when he burped himself right out of the ground. That old tree seemed bound and determined to keep him to herself.

Now he was clean with pale yellow paint dabbed with a bit of white. He recalled hearing muffled voices through the tightly growing shrubs in his old home. Now, similar voices were not muffled. He wondered where he would be tomorrow and hoped he wouldn't be returned to where he'd come from because Mrs. Maple was very stern and overbearing. The mailbox had little experience in the world, but certainly, Mrs. Maple had to be the most oppressive of her kind anywhere.

He remembered a little girl being his companion many years ago, but she hadn't been around for a long time, and he had loyally kept her treasures hidden.

15

As the sun rises each day, let it remind you to stretch your limbs and keep on walking, one step at a time.

Mrs. Sugar Maple – Twenty Years Previous

Dottie Johns was seven years old. She lived with her parents in a big old house outside of town. Her family was not a happy one. Her parents always argued. When they weren't arguing, they were detached. Dottie tried to be a good girl and not give them a reason to be mad, but it seemed that it wasn't enough, no matter what she did. The only place she found peace and contentment was in the woods, and her favorite place to hide was in the shrubs under the big old maple tree near the main road.

The tree was tall and broad, and the leaves were as big as dinner plates. The sap from the tree was sweet, and the tree shared with the girl. Dottie had cleared a small section in the shrubs and used that space as her private hideaway. It even had a mailbox. The mailbox had probably been used once upon a time, but as the years went by, it became obsolete, and now shrubs had grown around it, making it completely invisible from the road.

When Dottie first found it, a small key dangled from the lock. She opened it, to find a few letters that had never been claimed. She left them in the box and pretended in her play that it was important mail for her. She would thumb through the letters and pretend they were from relatives telling her about extraordinary adventures or that they were coming to visit for Christmas. Dottie would then plan elaborate family get-togethers.

She had a blanket she spread on the ground and would bring things from her mother's kitchen for picnic lunches. She never told anyone else about her secret place. It belonged to her, and she escaped to it whenever things got tough. She kept the little key on a string around her neck tucked under her shirt, and when things got scary at home, she would caress the key. It calmed her and helped her remember her peace under the tree's protective overhang.

The tree seemed to understand her, and when she came to play, it seemed to listen, and the breeze in the leaves sang lullabies. Often, Dottie had her most restful naps within the security of Old Mrs. Sugar Maple. The tree seemed to love bringing the little miss peace. Sometimes, leaves would fall and cover the child as a beautiful blanket. This worked exceptionally well in the late summer when the leaves turned various shades of orange, red, and yellow, mixed with a few green leaves that stubbornly refused to give up their chlorophyll.

When Dottie walked from her house to the maple tree, she sometimes went on the road and found treasures people had discarded. Once, she found a doll. Why would anyone throw away a doll? She took it to her special place and named it Sally. It became a part of her imaginary world where people spoke nicely to one another. Another time, she found a small bag, and when she opened it, she saw it had money. The money didn't look like anything she had seen before. She sounded out the word "Mexico" and decided to keep it if she ever went to Mexico. She took it to her special place, which became part of her and Sally's estate.

Old Mrs. Sugar Maple listened to the little girl as she played and knew that things were difficult for her when she wasn't beneath the expansive branches. She had even heard the little girl crying when she was scared. More than once, she saw little Dottie sitting on the ground sobbing her little heart out. Her knees were folded under her chin, her head buried in her knees.

Mrs. Sugar Maple was angry that someone was not kind to this sweet child. But the old tree was limited in how she could get involved. She could only keep the little girl safe when the child sought protection. The visits seemed to be happening more often and lasting longer.

Once, when it was dark and the little girl had fallen asleep, the maple tree heard a human voice calling out to Dottie. That is when Mrs. Maple learned the child's name. Dottie sprang to attention when she woke. But Dottie was hidden, crouched at the tree trunk, and remained very still. After the voice got further away, the little girl put the mail and the bag of Mexican money back in the box and locked it. She wrapped Sally in the blanket and laid her next to the trunk of the big tree. Then, she crept out of her hiding spot, went to the road, and called, "Mom, I'm right here. I just went for a walk. I'm sorry."

The woman scolded the little girl and told her never to walk on the highway again and to return home quickly. Mrs. Sugar Maple saw Dottie running up the road to the old Brooks house and her mother trailing behind with a determined, angry look. She even had a little switch in her hand that whistled in the wind when she shook it. Mrs. Maple thought that it was an odd thing to carry.

A few days later, Mrs. Sugar Maple saw the little girl in the back seat of a car with an attached trailer piled high with boxes pulling onto the main highway. When the vehicle stopped before entering the road, Dottie rolled down the window where she sat and called out, "Bye, Sally, I'll miss you." She waved, and Mrs. Sugar Maple heard the people in the front seat tell her to roll up the window and stop being silly. The little girl had tears rolling down her face as she settled back into her seat. Mrs. Maple never saw the child again and often wondered what had happened to her.

16

Remember to laugh often and love deeply.
These are the true riches of life.

The air was heavy with solemnity as friends and family gathered to bid farewell to Len Grant. The chapel was bathed in soft light, creating a tranquil ambiance. Organ music softly played hymns of hope and faith while the gathering mourners exchanged greetings in whispered reverence. Yet, amidst the grief, there was also a palpable feeling of love and devotion as those who knew Len came together to honor his memory.

The program would not be a lengthy one. Len never liked long meetings, and though he had nothing to say about this one, his family planned to honor his preferences.

Each of his children spoke to the congregation, recounting anecdotes and memories of their father. They testified about his kindness, wisdom, and unwavering love. They recalled his passion for gardening, poetry, and endless generosity toward others. Their voices blended in a chorus of remembrance. Each tale was met with nods of recognition and gentle smiles from mourners, a testament to Len's impact on those around him. Each memory was like a thread woven into the tapestry of Len's life, creating a vibrant portrait of the man they mutually loved and admired.

Even the littlest grandchildren participated by singing a song, "I Am a Child of God." The words were pronounced clearly and sweetly.

Hymns filled the chapel, offering moments of respite from the pain of loss. The familiar prayers and scriptures provided a sense of grounding, reminding everyone that Len's spirit lived on in the hearts of those he touched. In contrast, rituals provided comfort and solace to the grieving community.

As the service drew close, mourners were invited to pay their final respects to Len. Some approached the casket with tears streaming down their faces, while others stood in quiet contemplation. In this sacred space, grief was mingled with gratitude, and sorrow was tempered by the hope of seeing Len again in the eternities.

After the funeral services, the family reassembled at the cemetery where Len's last rites as a veteran were marked with an impressive three-volley gun salute, and the flag that covered his casket was reverently given to Dora with thanks for her husband's service. Each pallbearer left his boutonniere on the casket as a tribute. Dora, accompanied by her only son, approached the casket. She gently caressed it as her eyes filled with tears. His daughters likewise laid their hands on the casket and each whispered, "I love you, Daddy."

Following the service, friends and family gathered for a reception at the Grant home to honor Len's memory further and continue his family's support. The house was filled with laughter and conversation as people relaxed by sharing stories and reminiscing about their time with Len.

A table adorned with photographs and mementos served as a tribute to Len, offering a glimpse into the many facets of his personality and passions.

A slideshow of photographs played on a loop and offered a glimpse into his life, capturing moments of joy, laughter, and love. Images of family vacations, holiday gatherings, and everyday moments flashed across the screen, eliciting tears and smiles from those who watched. Each photograph was a snapshot of a life well-lived, a testament to the enduring bonds of love and friendship that Len cherished.

In one corner of the living room, a display ratified Len Grant's patriotism with pictures of him in his uniform, a flag he claimed while serving his country, and the uniform he wore as a soldier hanging in front of a portable screen. Service medals, plaques, and framed certificates completed the display.

The coffee table was covered with many poems that Len had written through the years. Clusters of guests exchanged stories about Len Grant, and as those stories unfolded, it became clear that Len's legacy extended far beyond his immediate family. He had touched the lives of countless people with his warmth and compassion, leaving an indelible mark on all who had the privilege of knowing him.

Of course, there was food, lots of food. People were very generous in providing sustenance for the Grant family.

Another thing in rich supply was the sense of camaraderie and solidarity as people came together to support one another in their grief. In this shared space, the hardship of loss felt a little lighter and the pain a little more bearable as they bore one another's burdens. As the afternoon wore on, it became clear that while Len may no longer inhabit a mortal body, his spirit lived in the hearts of all who knew and loved him.

Dora told her guests that she hoped in the days and weeks to come, her husband's legacy would continue to inspire acts of kindness, compassion, and love.

The day ended as signaled by the stars twinkling in the

evening sky. The Grant family took comfort in the knowledge that Len's light would continue shining brightly and guide them through the darkness, illuminating their paths with love. In the end, it is love that conquers all, and it is love that will ensure that Len's memory lives on for generations to come.

17

Live for today, like a bird on the wing;
Tomorrow will take care of itself.

Hannah's cab idled in the driveway while the meter ticked away, and the driver patiently waited. Hannah was determined to make one final plea to her mother about Brooks.

"Mother, I love you. I worry about all of us leaving you today." She hesitated and then continued, "I wish you could see that this whole bed-and-breakfast thing is folly. You don't need this kind of complication in your life. Look what it did to Daddy, he wasn't used to working like that, and now he's gone. Please sell the Brooks house, you have a lovely home right here. It's where we kids grew up. Enjoy retirement, go on a cruise, take classes at the college, volunteer at the hospital, or take up a hobby. There are plenty of things to keep you as busy as you want to be. I'm leaving here worried that you're going to work yourself to death. I'll help you find ways to invest your resources if you want, but not a bed-and-breakfast, it's beyond ridiculous."

Dora smiled weakly and hugged her daughter.

Hannah sighed and then walked out the door of her family home.

Dora stood in the doorway and waved a feeble goodbye, trying to smile even though her daughter's parting words ripped at her heart. She watched as her headstrong middle child oversaw the luggage being stowed and then stepped through the proffered cab door without a backward glance.

Dora felt like she had been punched in the gut, not literally, but every bit as debilitating.

"You don't mean that," Dora whispered, continuing her farewell wave.

Hannah appeared to be checking her phone and didn't look up as the car pulled away.

The new widow closed the door and wiped her face with her palms. The folds of her apron seemed a natural place to blot the moisture of tears. It wasn't the first time she had soaked in the blame for the death of her husband. She had insisted he slow down more than once, but he was so excited to create this bed-and-breakfast dream. Sometimes, he seemed driven beyond what Dora envisioned about the project. That was not an unfamiliar character trait. Len always jumped in with both feet when he took on a project.

Dora reminded herself that Len was a good man and always provided for his family. Yes, he was strong-willed, and it wasn't always easy to reason with him. "I feel fine," he always responded whenever she suggested he ease off. He seemed to find motivation on the other end of a hammer, saw, or shovel. He seemed determined that Brooks had something akin to a divine purpose, and he wanted to expose it for the benefit of guests.

Robyn and the children got away early this morning on a fifteen-hour flight back to Australia. Brian flew out separately for a meeting in Washington, DC. Eventually, he would join his family in their new assignment. Robyn was an Air Force officer's wife and a devoted mother. She loved her life as a bit of a gypsy going wherever the Air Force sent them.

Roger and his family left shortly after that. Dora had invited them to stay one more night and leave first thing in the morning, but Ann insisted they needed to be home to open the hardware store on time the next day.

"We've been gone a full week," she said. "We have a business to run."

Dora felt Ann's statements were pronounced with exclamation.

Roger's nod of silent agreement sealed the deal. The thirteen-year-old twin boys were in never-ending, mindless games on their phones. It didn't matter whether they were sitting in the back seat of the Dodge minivan or lounging at home as long as they had their electronics. The boys managed a quick hug as they spoke. Dora replayed the conversation in her head.

"Bye, Grandma, love you." Dora absently repeated the declaration to them as she muttered, "The Isolation Generation."

Roger's parting words were, "Call if you need anything and plan to visit us soon, we have an extra room."

Ann inherited the hardware store when her parents retired several years back. The retirees had been on the road since then, their reward for the many years they spent behind the counter of their store without vacations. Ann knew she was expected to maintain the family business. She grew up with it and knew it stem to stern. Roger left his job as a high school teacher to work the business, frequently professing enjoyment in his new career.

Hannah called her mother on the way to the airport with

what Dora considered a sham apology.

"I'm sorry, Mother, I shouldn't have jumped on you that way. I love you and support you just as you've always supported me. I'll call you later this week. We just pulled up to the departure area, so I have to go. Bye, Mother." Hannah hung up without waiting for a response.

Dora stared at the phone and then went to Len's office, where she stood in the doorway. Between all the hustle and bustle of the past week, Dora and Robyn had spent many hours learning the mechanics of information processing on the computer in Len's office. The young woman showed the technologically challenged older woman how to use a bookkeeping program for the new business. Dora recalled the strange way the computer had of announcing an incoming call and smiled.

It was an efficient room with a filing cabinet, a desk, and a comfortable chair on wheels. The computer sat front and center on the desk with a stapler, pencil sharpener, and container of writing implements, all within an arm's reach.

Len's favorite photo of the pair had them cuddling close together. It sat prominently on the desktop. Another photo was of Grandpa Len holding his youngest grandchild, little Lenny who had a particular fondness for his grandpa and sought out the lap of the old gentleman on any occasion. Len would carry the towheaded toddler around, talking to him like a grown-up. He told Lenny about the pictures on the wall and how they would go fishing someday, and he encouraged the boy always to try hard to do the right thing.

"Grumpy," Lenny had proclaimed boldly, "I love you."

Len responded with a trumped-up look of puzzlement, gazing into the innocent face of youth, "Why do you love Grampy?"

The little boy hesitantly answered, "I don't got no reason, Grumpy, I just do."

The toddler's mom heard the whole exchange, snapped the picture, and then rehearsed the conversation with the family. Dora remembered how, days later, Len laughed when Robyn gave him the framed photo while reminding him of the sweet exchange. He had since told the story a dozen times to anyone who would listen.

It wasn't lost on the family that the child called his grandpa "Grumpy." It wasn't meant disrespectfully. It was just the charm of baby talk.

Dora would miss those up close and personal exchanges. Still, according to Robyn, technology would ensure that the children knew their grandparents through video calls.

When Len died, Roger and his family were the first to arrive at the family home. They thankfully took over the details of calling the mortuary and notifying family and friends. The next several days were filled with meetings, funeral planning, and decision-making. But the evenings were glorious and even therapeutic. The whole family gathered after dinner each night and reveled in family stories. These hours were like a healing salve. It had been a week and a day since then. It was sudden, and life in the Grant household had been a whirlwind of activity since.

This was Dora's first experience with the death of a close relative. She never knew her father. Her mother, Eva, was in an independent living center nearby and, as a feisty older woman, could run circles around Dora and her friends in the home where she lived. She raised her only daughter by herself and did pretty well despite herself. That declaration was always followed with a loud laugh.

Dora's only aunt was her mother's sister, and Dora was still a child when Aunt Becca died, childless and widowed.

In retrospect, the past week had flown by just like the last forty-five years of marriage had disappeared. The pair were no more than kids when they began adult life as a married duo after Len left the Army. They were full of idealism, dreams, and love. It became apparent in the intervening years that their dreams would need to be harnessed as they dealt with reality. Children needed attention, a career needed nourishment, and marriage required maintenance. Life sometimes felt like a runaway horse, and the best way to keep a seat was to hold on for dear life.

Things slowed down. Their family responsibilities lessened, and the conclusion of Len's career loomed. Then they decided to look for something else, and it didn't take long for Len to present to Dora what he termed the *perfect opportunity*. It presented itself in the framework of his old family home lovingly called Brooks. He had pointed out, "It would be an amazing location for a bed-and-breakfast."

She suspected it was an idea that had percolated for an extended period.

"It'll be a retreat for tired executives, a private place for lovers, a place for newlyweds to create memories, a place for families to start traditions," he had pleaded and added almost apologetically, "There's some much-needed work to be done." He then somberly nodded his head and, in the same breath, added, "I'm amazed at how well it's withstood the test of time, Dora." With contagious excitement in his voice, he had looked hopefully at his wife, trusting he had convinced her to jump on board.

The memory was encased in tears finding their way down Dora's jawline as she pictured Len wearing his leather carpentry apron, a gift from their son, Roger, who said he was proud of his parents. He even offered to lend time to help with work needing to be done on the grand old house.

For now, Dora was tired, perhaps exhausted from dealing with all the realities of her precarious balance near the top rung of the ladder of life. She happily remembered the first time she saw the property. Len had pointed out birds building nests in tree branches, chipmunks hiding food, and bugs inhabiting rotted tree stumps. It was all within the forest of trees with many gurgling streams.

Dora was healthy and in pretty good shape for a woman in the shadows of seventy. Still, she was also scared by the realization that she had never been alone. Three younger sisters ensured Dora would grow up sharing everything, including a bed. The night before her wedding, she slept in the same bed as her younger sister in a room they shared with two more sisters. The next night, she shared a bed with her husband.

Now, she was alone. The grandfather clock in the living room started a familiar reminder of time passing. Subconsciously, Dora counted the chimes: one, two, three, four, five, six, seven. From the reclining chair where she sat, she stared out the big bay window onto a grassy, flourishing backyard so tenderly cared for by a man no longer mortal. She watched as the light of day gave way to the obscurity of darkness. The chair to her side was painfully empty. There seemed to be an indentation where Len's form typically stretched out. She recalled that the guests avoided his chair throughout the day, even when the house was full of well-wishers. Even the teenagers, so full of themselves, seemed to understand that a part of Grandpa Len should remain in the house undisturbed.

Friends, family, and neighbors returned to their everyday lives. By now, they were all watching television news, preparing bowls of popcorn, and laughing while planning activities for the coming day. In a few hours, they would brush their teeth, say their prayers, and climb into beds.

However, Dora was alone.

Silence.

She wondered, had it always been this quiet?

Gradually, night-lights illuminated throughout the house. Dora felt safe in the home she shared with Len for almost half their married lives. This time last month, he sat in his recliner with his feet propped up. He sported a sports cap perched over his forehead with the brim shading his resting eyes. At this time of night, the only noise came from the customary audio of the television. He was a quiet napper, but the television was always on, usually an old black-and-white western. The Brooks' place gave Len reason to leave the chair and don his carpenter garb. He said he loved doing it, but now he was gone.

Dora felt drained, but it was too early to go to bed. The house was clean, even the kitchen, every crumb and morsel wiped away, the dishwasher loaded and unloaded, the floors swept clean, and the rugs bore line marks where the vacuum proved its worth. The pillows on the couches were fluffed, and someone even indented each pillow as though staging a house showing.

I'm glad I asked them not to touch our bedroom.

Flower arrangements from the funeral were scattered throughout the house, some looking droopy. The number of red, white, and blue arrangements attested to those who knew Len as a patriotic veteran. He was also a dedicated gardener and would only partially approve of the cut flowers honoring his life. He preferred to enjoy plants in their natural habitat, outside, attached to the ground by a robust root system. That's one of the reasons his love of the old family home had remained strong. The five acres of plant life put him into an overload of nature appreciation. Dora closed her eyes and remembered how she had felt Brooks' sacred peacefulness.

She must have fallen asleep because chimes aroused her daydreams, and a glance at the clock on the television receiver confirmed it to be bedtime. Moisture had collected in the corner of her mouth and threatened to trickle down her chin. She wiped it with the edge of her apron. Dora returned the recliner to its upright position, pulled herself out of the chair, and went to the kitchen. She took a glass from the cupboard, filled it with water, and carried it to her empty bedroom.

She looked at the same unaltered furniture arrangement, the same house shoes beside his side of the bed, the medicine vials stacked neatly on the bedside table, and the same lamp set square in the middle with a box of tissues nearby. The small waste can was filled with wadded-up tissues and tucked next to the bed. She stared benumbed, then moved mechanically to place the glass of water on her bedside table.

She had always shared the single sink of the ensuite bathroom, but now, she stood directly in front of it, staring at two toothbrushes on the stand. His bath towel still hung rumpled on the towel rod, not damp. It was all a reflection of the many details of the life of Len Grant.

"Tomorrow," she uttered to her reflection in the mirror.

Dora returned to her side of the bed, turned off the lamp, adjusted her pillow, and slipped under the sheets. This time last month, Len would reach for her hand, and they would fall asleep that way, not tonight, not ever again.

Once more, Dora's eyes clouded and then flooded with tears for everything she had endured in the yesterdays and now for everything she had reason to fear in the tomorrow.

Tomorrow, Dora would plan.

Tomorrow, she would tackle the bills, the insurance, and the technicalities involved in finalizing the ending of a well-lived life.

Tomorrow would be her time to figure out what needed to be done. For now, she was in bed and would sleep off this chapter of her life, awakening to a new chapter.

Tomorrow she would live alone.

18

Keep the faith like a sturdy oak; It'll weather.

Dora's sleep was abruptly interrupted by the roar of a diesel engine and barking dogs. She pulled off her sleep mask, and her eyes were assaulted with piercing light through plantation shutters.

Ugh, garbage day.

The visual of stuffed-to-the-brim receptacles filled her mind, and she jumped out of bed. She donned a pair of sweatpants, a T-shirt, and jammed her feet into slip-ons. Len usually had this chore.

Things were different now.

After a week of extra people, the cans were almost overflowing. She dragged each to the curb just in time for the pickup, then lugged them back to their station at the side of the house. From now on, she would likely be using but one can, and sadness filled her heart.

This time, a month ago, her mind relished the idea of becoming an innkeeper, an entrepreneur. She and Len had spent hours discussing niceties they would have for their guests and how they would advertise their new endeavor. Their relationship had always been good, but with this new adventure, it seemed to multiply and flourish like the flowers Len loved.

Her new role would be very different from her duties as chief cook and bottle washer of the Grant household. Through the years, she had occasionally enjoyed having a few people in her home and didn't mind cooking, while preparing for a night of exciting conversation. Now, she was mistress of the house. Len had referred to his role as the CEO of Brooks Bed & Breakfast. Dora didn't know what that acronym entailed, but it didn't sound like anything she saw herself doing. She was sure it included being a bookkeeper of some sort and knew that was something she definitely didn't want to do. She loved being with people and quickly saw herself as the hostess, that part would be fun.

She shivered a little, realizing she would now do both jobs alone.

Dora decided to sit on the porch swing for a bit. Her mind wandered as she looked up at the clear sky and the promise of a warm, pleasant day. It was quiet, and from her chair she could see the main road. A few joggers and walkers strained at the leashes of their animals. The world was coming alive like it was any normal day. Her neighbor across the street left his house, waved, and got in his truck. Dora waved back and took a deep breath. She forced herself to get out of the swing. It was not a normal day for her.

Maybe later this afternoon, she would take one of the many bouquets scattered throughout the house and freshen up the small plot of land dedicated to the memory of her husband. She had much to do and didn't have time to dawdle in self-pity or even grieve too long. People had cautioned her that grief had its timeline and to allow herself to get through it at whatever pace she needed. It would run a parallel timeline while she learned to conduct a business.

Dora went to the kitchen, poured herself a tall glass of energy from the container of orange juice, and carried it to the office.

She picked up the to-do list Roger had made for her. The list was long, with mundane things that represented the nuts and bolts of Len's life—cancel his phone, gym membership, and some magazine subscriptions. There were insurance policies, credit cards, and probably some unpaid bills. So many tedious details making up one person's everyday existence. A summation of Len Grant's life and ending with a death certificate.

Len had a looseleaf binder marked Finances. Dora knew she would have to tackle it page by page. Though the big picture was daunting, she would deal with each chunk, one step at a time.

Everything in his office had a place, that was so Len. Distinctive service plaques hung on the wall representative of his military service and career as a postal worker. The bookcase held stacks of gardening magazines with dog-eared pages and his favorite novels, including an excessive number of Louis L'Amour paperbacks.

Fortunately, Len had left his internet passwords readily accessible. Roger advised her to change them and to secure the new ones someplace safe, and not just a piece of paper. Time to get down to business. She opened the finance binder, picked up a packet of yellow sticky notes, and dove in where Len had left off. She hoped.

This was new territory for Dora. She picked up her phone and dialed the first number on her list.

Three hours later, Dora sat silently at the desk, gazing at stacks of papers, each topped with a sticky yellow note noting a problem. She stared out the window, wanting to detach from the reality of what had gelled in the last couple of hours. Dora had always been content to leave the finances to Len, and he repeatedly assured her of its well-being.

"Things are great. It would be best if you didn't worry about a thing," he had said.

They never discussed the intricacies of money management. In truth, Dora didn't want to be involved in that aspect of their life, and it seemed that Len probably didn't want her involved. Dora was content to care for their house and children and to plan family activities. Len always gave her a household allowance and never questioned how it was spent. She had a lovely home, and there always seemed to be money for vacations and gifts. She was not a spendthrift and practiced a frugal household. She watched for sales, learned to cook from scratch, and ensured the children were happy and cared for. That was her bailiwick, and she joyfully embraced it.

But now, she sat at the massive desk while her head thumped like a driven spike pounded into a debt coffin.

"How could he do this to me," she angrily whispered.

It was as though she was drowning in a giant muddy river of sludge as spinning dollar signs splatted the pristine walls of her place of refuge. She picked up the picture of a smiling couple on Len's desk and plaintively asked a question.

"How am I going to fix this?"

Her sigh was labored.

Dora, you are smart, capable, and you can do this. Figure it out.

She recalled a quote from Albert Einstein, "It's not that I'm so smart. It's just that I stay with problems longer."

Dora had more than one problem, none would just disappear. She was tenacious and would take time to think through each one. Her ringing phone brought her back to reality, and after the fourth ring, she answered. Despite her newly proclaimed confidence, she barely got out the words to greet the caller.

"Hello."

"Good morning, Dora. How are you doing today?"

It was Jean, her close friend. She felt soothed but mumbled, "I'm okay, I guess."

"I can come over. It'll only take a few minutes."

"Oh, Jean, I'm sorry. I've been busy all morning with some bookkeeping, and I'm a little upset. I'll be okay. I don't want to bother you with anything."

"It's no bother. I think we both need some downtime. I know the kids left yesterday, and I figured you might want some company. It's almost time for lunch. I'll pick something up at Kravers for the two of us."

"That sounds good, thank you, Jean."

Jean went on, "I've never seen Brooks. Why don't I pick you up, and we'll take our lunch there for a picnic."

Dora didn't respond right away. She didn't want to bare her soul and always felt obligated never to burden anyone with personal problems. She knew others had their difficulties as well.

"What do ya say?" Jean asked again.

"Uh, yeah, I guess we can do that. I'm tired of all these papers anyway. I'll take a quick shower and be ready in a few."

"Okay, see you soon."

Dora hung up and pushed away from the desk, her vision fixed on the stacks representing the shambles of her resources. She closed her eyes and, with a slight shake of her head, arose from her seat and walked away.

"I've got to make some serious life changes," she whispered as she touched the rings encircling the third finger of her left hand.

Dora got dressed, and she thought about the last time she and Len visited Brooks.

They had wandered the forest surrounding the grand old house. Len was in his element then, and orated like a botany professor, educating Dora with names of flora and fauna. He was a self-taught herbalist and believed in using nature to its full advantage. He learned new and exciting ways to effectively treat and cure everyday ills with what he referred to as *his sacred medicine cabinet*.

"That's what God intended," he had declared.

Len loved the small forest animal life abounding amongst the verdant greenery. They had watched rabbits skittering from bush to bush, squirrels and chipmunks scampering up tree trunks, and deer languishing in their protected areas, quietly nibbling grass. He had shown Dora animal tracks around small creeks teeming with fish, and he rehearsed his plans for a glorious flower garden on the property.

"I want to plant hyacinths. Did you know their fragrance is caught before you ever see the flower, and they're the best evidence of the arrival of spring," he had declared. "Peonies usually bloom just in time for Memorial Day, and they seem as big as a summer sunset."

He pointed to where he would put magnolias, dahlias, and hollyhocks. He told her, "The hollyhocks remind me of my grandma. The colors looked like they came from a painter's palette."

Len wanted their guests to experience the healing powers of nature. He put sensory stations in five different locations within the forest behind Brooks. He wanted people to have a place to sit and ponder where they could focus on nature, without worldly distractions. "People need time to examine their souls," he had said. "They'll come away with a better appreciation of self and the beautiful world we share with other life forms."

He also intended to have a working garden planted from seed.

He said it would be a testament of hope as tiny sprouts popped out of the ground, grew, and became nourishing, life-giving food. He wanted to landscape with flowers and herbs and hang bird feeders near the windows. He said the fruit tree orchard would be protected and maintained, and he wanted to add window boxes filled with colorful blooms. He also planned a prayer garden with signs focusing on the Beatitudes Christ taught in the Sermon on the Mount. This would be where a prominent sign would be hung quoting Len's favorite Bible verse from the book of Job:

> But ask now the beasts, and they shall teach thee; and the fowls of the air, and they shall tell thee: Or speak to the earth, and it shall teach thee: and the fishes of the sea shall declare unto thee. Who knoweth not in all these that the hand of the Lord hath wrought this? In whose hand is the soul of every living thing and the breath of all humanity. – Job 12:7-10

Even now, with everything upsetting she had learned this morning, Dora couldn't help but smile as she remembered her husband's enthusiasm, genuine love of nature, and flight of fancy for Brooks.

"What am I supposed to do now?" she asked.

"Oh, Len," she whimpered as she crumpled to her knees and longed for his arms to hold her and make this all go away.

19

Take time to sit and ponder,
like a cow chewing cud under the shade.

Jean gave Dora a quick hug. "Good morning, sunshine, how are you today, anyway?" A few inches shorter than Dora, Jean's sturdy frame was robust as her boisterous laugh.

Dora returned her friend's hug. "I'm good."

"I'm looking forward to meeting Brooks."

"I'm excited to show it to you, let me grab my bag. I have a mailbox to take back to Brooks." Dora gathered her things. "Do you want some water?"

"Sure, but I've got drinks and sandwiches for a picnic. I stopped at Kravers Deli and got us Reubens."

"Okay, I'm right behind you."

"That's a cute little mailbox, what's it's story?"

"Roger found it when he was clearing out the overgrowth around the maple tree at the entry, and Ann cleaned it up and repainted it. There's something inside of it, but it's locked. I'm hoping to run across a key."

As usual, Jean's red Toyota Camry was littered with junk mail and a few fast-food sacks. She hurried ahead and cleared the passenger side of her vehicle.

"Sorry, I should have done this before I left home. I guess I shouldn't have left all this stuff here." Jean stuffed everything in a grocery store plastic bag she had no trouble locating amongst the litter.

Dora slid into the seat and closed the door.

"Okay, we're off. I think I know the way. I've often driven past that old house and always wondered about it. I'm excited to get a personal tour finally."

Jean continued to talk and laugh.

Dora smiled and occasionally gave an obligatory nod accompanied by a smile, hoping to communicate that she might be listening.

"Dora, Dora, are you in there," Jean asked. "This is the turn-off, right?"

"Oh, yes. Sorry, Jean. I guess I got lost in my thoughts. My landmark is the big old sugar maple tree, I barely recognize it. Roger spearheaded a work project clearing out the overgrowth. When you round the bend ahead, you'll see the house."

The well-packed graveled road was wide enough for two cars. Jean carefully steered, and soon, the house amid a forest of trees and shrubs came into view. A small parking lot was on one side of the structure, but the road naturally turned into a wide circular driveway where Jean stopped the car in front of the entry.

"Can we park here, or do you want me to park in the lot?"

"We can park here. I'm not expecting anyone." Dora unbuckled her seat belt and opened the car door.

"Dora, grab that blanket in the back seat. We'll use it for our picnic."

Dora put her purse on her shoulder and got the blanket and the mailbox while Jean collected the sandwich bags and drink holder. She followed Dora to the front door. A "Welcome to Brooks" porch mat greeted their arrival.

The house key appeared to be made of brass with a delicate filigree pattern at its head and dangled from a long yellow cord. Dora had suggested to Len they have the house upgraded with new locks, but he insisted that the present system be maintained since it was all part of the house's charm. He wanted to keep everything intact.

Dora put the aged key in the lock of the massive oak door and, with a careful turn, heard it disengage. She pushed against the door, and it swung open to a stately entry and enchanting interior. The door hung from wrought iron hinges, perhaps forged on the on-site shop's blacksmith anvil.

The women took some time wandering through the house and admiring the artistry.

Dora explained, "The house was built in the early 1900s, and Len's family has owned it for over one hundred years. They lived in it most of those years, but it's been empty for the last twenty. Len inherited it, but it's been in probate for a long time. The furniture is all original, and we've kept up basic repairs and general cleaning. It's so beautiful, I love it. I feel like I belong here even as an in-law."

Jean seemed captivated. "I've never seen anything like it."

Dora smiled. "Me either."

The house had a sophisticated, homey vibe, from the arched doors to the sturdy, solid brick hearths. Most walls were troweled with textured plaster, some were wallpapered.

Dora sighed as she wandered into a parlor-type room, its walls covered with a floral print. Her fingers grazed the wallpaper, a touch that felt as intimate as connecting with the fingerprints of those who had come before her. She and Jean went to the library, Len's favorite room, where floor-to-ceiling shelves were filled with books. It naturally invited readers to settle into one of several nooks with a book in hand. The scent of ancient parchment filled the air, mingling with the faint aroma of fading ink.

Breathing out the words, Dora said, "You've got to see the grounds. It's so peaceful. Follow me."

Their footsteps resonated in the quiet chambers as they walked down the hall to the kitchen. Stark-white kitchen walls met an equally white ceiling hovering over immaculate classic checkerboard flooring, a 1950s Wedgewood stove, and beautiful brush-painted cabinets.

The workstation included a farmer's sink with porcelain lever handles, a swing-spout faucet, and an attached soap dish. It was framed by a window offering an unobstructed view of the gardens.

Dora turned the decorative doorknob of the hefty back door and proceeded through a small screened-in porch.

The *Sensory Station of Touch* flourished with greenery and beckoned guests to come closer and the gurgles of a nearby stream lured them. Dora spread the blanket next to the stream, and as she and Len had done previously, she removed her shoes to commune with the sacred ground. Her bare feet sunk into the soft grass, and she felt a tingling of familiarity, a serenity, a rapport with nature.

Jean closed her eyes and did likewise.

Dora seemed to be lost in a trance, so Jean fixed their plates of a sandwich and chips. She pulled two drinks from the cooler.

Jean waved a hand in front of her friend's face. "Dora, let's have lunch, and I want to hear about this house."

Dora turned to the voice of her friend and smiled. The angst she had felt about Len's loss that had consumed her thoughts all morning had lost its place.

"I know it's hard for you right now with Len's death and all, but you do have so much to be grateful for. I envy you—in a good way. You have your kids, grandkids, a lovely home, and now all this."

"I am blessed, I can't deny that. I guess I just didn't see my life without Len…so soon."

The two women were silent for several minutes.

Finally, Jean asked, "Are you okay?"

Dora nodded. "Yeah, I'm good. I haven't eaten much the last few days—I'm starving." She tore open the bag of chips, unwrapped the sandwich, and took a bite.

Jean laughed. "There's the Dora I know. What gives anyway? You seemed upset when I called this morning, and you've been out of touch since I picked you up. Now, all of a sudden, you seem like the old Dora. What's going on?"

Dora looked her friend in the eyes, shook her head, and took a deep breath.

"I feel at peace, and honestly, I don't understand it. For some reason, my troubles seem more manageable here. Len said it was the harmony of nature and that Brooks always brings out the best in people." She took a drink of water. "I'm in trouble, Jean. I've discovered that Len neglected to tell me many things about our financces, and *I am in trouble.*"

Jean's eyes widened. "And?"

Dora sighed, trying to ward off the words gathering in her brain, not sure she wanted them to find their way to her tongue.

Finally, she said, "Hold on to your hat because this is a wild ride. I thought our house was paid off, but it has a mortgage on it. Len's life insurance policy and his 401K plan both have loans against them, and three credit cards have been maxed out. I don't know what Len had in mind for managing all this debt because he never told me anything. You, Jean, are looking at a woman who is up to her eyeballs in debt. Plus, I have no skills equal to the kind of job I need to earn an adequate salary. Remember, I'm sixty-eight years old. What do I do?"

"Wow, how are you not screaming your lungs out?"

"I did all that a few hours ago. I was amid a crying jag when you called, and I've been numb since. But, for some reason, now I feel calm, even at peace. It's confusing."

"I knew something was wrong, but I never dreamed it was like this. I thought you were grieving for Len."

"That's why I'm so bewildered, Jean. I'm honestly a little lost at the prospect of being alone, and I miss him every minute, and then I'm so mad I could spit that he left me in such a mess. Len always took care of things. He was always a faithful husband, a good father, an adequate provider, and an all-around good man. I never had a clue that we couldn't afford all *this*." She threw her arms open. "He assured me he had it all worked out. This kind of irresponsibility was not like him."

The bench was new to the communication in the forest, and he watched as trees and shrubs leaned into the conversation. Even the house sullenly expressed worry with groans coming through its settling floors.

Dora shrugged her shoulders in submission, and Jean put a comforting arm around her.

"Look, I have some money saved. You're welcome to whatever might help. Honest, I love you, Dora. I want to help."

"No, we're the same age, and you need your money. I wouldn't think of using any of it."

"Well, actually, you're older than me, remember?" The corner of Jean's mouth turned up at the banter about their age difference.

Dora chuckled. "Right, I keep forgetting about that three-month age difference, and need I remind you to respect your elders?"

"I don't want to see you standing on some street corner holding a sign. Seriously, Dora, if you need money to tide you over while you work this out, don't hesitate to ask."

"Stop it," Dora scolded. "Finish your lunch, and then I'll take you upstairs. You've got to see the bedrooms. Wait until you see the quilts we found in the attic, they're all spectacular."

They gathered the picnic remains and went back into the house and up the stairs.

Dora pointed out the bedrooms, two with ensuite bathrooms. "There's a third bathroom and it's meant to be shared by occupants of the other two bedrooms."

Each bed was covered with a handmade quilt and matching shams.

The quilt in the main bedroom had something reminiscent of Vincent van Gogh's famous painting. It captured the magic of a clear night sky filled with twinkling stars. Dark blue fabric served as the backdrop for a celestial scene with appliqued stars of various sizes scattered across the quilt surface. Metallic thread accents added shimmer and depth to the starry expanse while quilted swirls and crescent moons danced among the constellations. It was a celestial masterpiece.

One quilt featured cascades of roses in soft pastel hues, each meticulously pieced together from various patterned fabrics, creating a charming patchwork effect.

Another seemed inspired by the rugged beauty of the natural world. It was in shades of green, brown, and gray, with quilted motifs of pine trees, wildlife, and meandering streams bringing the wilderness to life.

The last quilt seemed to capture the warm hues of a sunset over rolling hills. The patchwork design featured rich oranges, deep reds, and golden yellows. It was ablaze with color and had intricate stitching outlining the quilt blocks, depicting silhouettes of trees and birds against the fading light.

"Oh, Dora, you were right, those quilts are exquisite, and that main bedroom is gorgeous. My mom was a quilter. I have a few of her masterpieces, and I love them. This place is going to be very popular."

The women continued talking as they went down the stairs.

"That was the plan. There's one more small bedroom downstairs off the kitchen. I think it might have been used for live-in help. It's crossed my mind that I could live in that one and maybe rent out my house in town to help with my financial predicament. Besides, it would be handy to live on-site."

"That's a good idea. See, you're figuring things out. You're going to be fine."

They walked to the front entry. "Hey, what's this?" asked Jean. "I didn't notice this when we came in."

In the corner by the hall closet sat a cardboard box.

"That must be the box Len told me about. He found a trunk in the attic with stuff he thought we might use on our history wall. I guess Mr. Lowry, down the road, is refurbishing the trunk, so Len put the contents in a cardboard box. He asked me to sort through it and decide what we wanted to keep."

"Here," Jean said. "Take my bag, and I'll put the box in my car. We can go through it at your place. Maybe it will lead us to a buried treasure, and all your worries will be over," she said with a playful grin.

Dora rolled her eyes. "Yeah, that's probably exactly what will happen. I've got cheesecake at home. Want some dessert?"

"You know I have a sweet tooth, and I love cheesecake. Do you have any blueberry topping?"

"Umm, maybe."

Have you ever heard the term, *Oh, to be a fly on the wall?*

Brooks and his entourage are like a fly infestation as they digest the overheard conversation. They sensed a hurt, sadness, and an unwelcome fear from Dora. They wanted to inspire her to realize that when fear creeps in, another presence known as challenge looms ahead. Gut toughness isn't about denying fear. It's about facing it head on. It's acknowledging the nerves and pushing forward anyway with the determination to tackle whatever comes despite trembling hands and a racing heart. True strength is found in the grit to keep going, even when every instinct screams to turn back. It's about meeting fear with a steely resolve and refusing to let it hold you back. Ultimately, it's not about being fearless but tough enough to confront your fears and rise to the challenge.

20

*Slow down and enjoy the ride
like a lazy river winding through the hills.*

Jean parked her car in the driveway of Dora's home, and the pair went inside with Jean carrying the cardboard box.

"It's amazing how much contrast there is in the outside temperature at Brooks and what we have here in the city," said Dora. "I suppose having all the trees and running water makes a big difference."

"You're probably right." Jean placed the cardboard box on a large stool near the kitchen countertop. "Would you like to do the honors, missy?"

"I'm going to dish up cheesecake. You go ahead. I can see by the glint in your eyes how much you want to."

With one fell swoop, Jean got a knife from the kitchen drawer and slit the top open. She peered inside while Dora prepared their desserts, occasionally glancing at Jean rifling through the treasure chest's contents.

"Finding anything interesting?"

"Oh, Dora, look at this quilt top. I recognize this pattern

with the barn motif in the middle. The surrounding shades of yellow and green are meant to resemble fields of golden wheat and green pastures. My mother made one similar to it. She called Grandpa's Barn."

She handed the quilt top to Dora, who took it to the sofa, spread it over the back cushions, and then stood back to admire it fully.

"These days, people sew quilts with machines. I'll bet those at Brooks were done by hand and took days to complete." Jean reached into the box and pulled out a stack of booklets tied with string. She set them on the counter, loosened the string, and fanned them out.

Dora walked over to the counter. "What are those?"

"Looks like owner manuals for small appliances. I'll bet most of these things have long been trashed. I'll help you do a bit of an audit to see what's useable."

"I want to keep everything that is salvageable. Len recognized a unique charm about Brooks and wanted to maintain that appeal. You know, the more I think about it, the more I agree with his philosophy. The house is an original, and there's a distinction about it I can't deny. Somehow, it feels disrespectful to toss things away for something new."

"Yeah, you're right. But it would be best if you also thought about efficiency. If you're going to run a bed-and-breakfast, the wise use of your time in meal preparation ought to be considered. Hey, do you intend on doing all the housework and cooking for this business yourself?"

"I want to be involved, but I recognize it's a big job. I'm hoping I can hire out some of the work. It would be ideal to have someone help with the cooking, housekeeping, and of course a groundskeeper. Hopefully I can find people as dedicated to Brooks as Len was, who would see it as not just a job, but a privilege to care for a *resplendent edifice*. That's how Len referred to Brooks." She turned to her friend. "Are you available?"

"You know I'd do anything I could to help you, but honestly, I don't need another job. I'm at the stage where I don't even like my job. I'm considering retirement."

"I understand, I hope that works out because you deserve to have some serious downtime."

Jean held up a roll of paper. "This might be interesting. It's probably blueprints for the house. That's something you'll want to keep."

Dora cleared a section of the countertop and rolled out the multi-page drawings, holding them open briefly. Her attention was diverted when Jean pulled out a leather-bound notebook. With a snap, the blueprints returned to their original rolled form, and Dora set them aside. She took the notebook from Jean and opened it.

"It's filled with dated notes from 1910, and I think its entries are the daily progress of the build. This could be fun to read." She opened the notebook to a random page and read, "'Brought windows—the fields of grain sway. I'm told it is called float glass.' How lovely."

Dora looked up from the notebook. "I need to google 'float glass.' I wonder what that means?" She continued to thumb through a few more pages. "I love old cursive handwriting. There's an artistry about it that entrances me."

Jean was immersed in another item she lifted from the box with great care. She handed Dora a small wooden box. "Here, you open this one."

The cover of the box was attached with leather strap hinges. A carved intricate filigree pattern adorned the top, similar to that on the front door key. The grain of the wood swirled like the current of a small stream, and it had smooth, sanded corners. The entire box was polished to a high luster. She carefully opened it, set it on the counter, and delicately picked a trinket from its interior.

"Oh, Jean, look at this."

Dora's fingers held an exquisite, polished heart-shaped stone, wrapped in a nest of twisted wire dangling from a silver chain. The initials "BG" was etched on the stone.

"BG—I wonder who it belonged to? It looks like nothing more than a polished rock. The setting is unusual, rather rustic, and probably not valuable. Still, someone found it valuable enough to do a lot of work to show it off."

Jean asked, "What was Len's grandmother's name?"

"I saw it in that little notebook about the house being built. Let's see …"

Dora found the notebook and opened the cover. "Here it is. Of course, her name was Beth Grant."

"Well then," said Jean, "that mystery is solved. It's an interesting piece of jewelry. I'd wear it if I were you."

"Yeah, I think I will. I knew Len's parents, Pete and Emma Grant. They were wonderful people, but I want to find out more about Timothy and Beth Grant. They built Brooks, and I think there's something significant hidden in the walls of that house, figuratively speaking. Len tried to explain it to me more than once. He could be very philosophical sometimes. Len was what some call a Renaissance man. He didn't graduate from college, but he was well-educated." She smiled. "Len was charming, witty, and loved to dance. Did you know he wrote poetry and had a pretty good singing voice? I have a notebook filled with poems he wrote."

She clasped the necklace around her neck, lovingly touched the stone, and then admired how it rested against her skin.

"On the other hand, he would wrestle with the kids, and I'm

sure my man could probably fight like a swordsman if he had to. I would get lost in the sound of his voice."

Jean cut short the reminiscence.

"Here's another key. I wonder what it's for?" She held a small brass key between her fingers. It had the same filigree pattern as on the front door key and the small wood box. Dora took the front door key out of her pocket and held it next to the smaller one. They were similar except for the leather fob on the little key instead of the long yellow plastic cord on the house key.

"Another mystery," Dora said, placing both keys on the counter. "Wait a minute. Remember the mailbox we took out to Brooks this morning? I'll bet this key belongs to it. I'll try it the next time I go out there. I'm dying to find out what is rattling inside it."

She then eyed a small metal-looking object atop a stack of papers and carefully lifted it out. It appeared to be a picture but was slightly flexible and had an almost mirror-like surface. The couple in the picture had pleasant looks on their faces but not exactly smiling. The man was tall, lean, and wore a suit with a vest, a white shirt, and a bow tie. The collars on his shirt stood up with wing tips folded back, and he wore a white fedora with a black band above the brim. He had kind eyes and a full mustache.

The lady's dress was long-sleeved and had a modest neckline. It was cinched at the waist with a wide belt. She wore a necklace, and her hat appeared to be made of straw and was adorned with what was likely a colorful array of flowers. It was easy to imagine despite the picture resembling an X-ray. There was a familiarity about them suggesting they were a married couple as they stood in front of Brooks.

"I wonder?" Dora whispered. She put the picture down and hurried out of the room.

"Hey, where are you off to?"

"I'll be right back."

Within minutes, Dora reappeared with a picture album in her arms and placed it on the counter. She opened it and thumbed through the pages, stopping on a page with a picture of a couple in front of a house.

"Jean, look. I have the same picture, but it's glossy." She picked up the relic.

"These are Len's grandparents, Timothy and Beth Grant. They built Brooks in 1910. My glossy has better details, but tintype pictures are rare. I think the necklace she's wearing is the same one as I have here."

Dora delicately placed the tintype on the counter before returning to the small treasure chest. She picked up an envelope and recognized Len's handwriting on the outside. Inside the envelope were two folded pieces of paper. One crackled as she opened it, and the other appeared to be a duplicate created more recently.

"These are maps, and this one is in Len's handwriting." She pointed to the words *Bench Placement* at the top of both maps. There are five spots, each marked with an 'x.' "This map of Brooks' gardens shows where Len and Roger put those sensory reflection benches. You remember, like the one where we had our picnic today?"

Dora and Jean studied the drawings.

"I think you're right, Dora. Look, that is the house, and then beyond, you can see a fence line, and out here on the edges, those little curly lines are probably the creeks you told me about. We need to go back with this map and find each of the 'x-marked spots.' This is going to be our next big adventure."

"There's plenty of time for adventure, Jean. And you will be the first person I think of when I decide to solve the mystery of the 'x's.' Is there anything else in there?"

"Yeah, more papers, some odds and ends. Here's an envelope. It's not old, but there's something in it."

Jean handed Dora the small, sealed envelope.

Dora opened it and pulled out a flat key with very defined edges, and a page with a few lines of writing. It seemed familiar, yet nothing she could instantly identify.

"We have yet another key and another mystery," said Jean.

Dora quietly read the lines of writing, "Box two thirty-nine, Mondale Bank."

"What does that mean?"

"Our bank is in Mondale, but I don't know what Box two thirty-nine is. You know what, Brooks' mailing address is two thirty-nine Grouse Road. The bank is closed for the weekend, but I'll put that on my list for Monday morning."

Jean laughed. "This just gets better and better."

"Yeah," whispered Dora. "I need that cheesecake. I'll finish going through this stuff later. You are welcome to stay and watch TV or read, but I'm going to get busy with some creative financing."

21

"As you journey through life's winding road, remember to dance with the changes, for they bring the sweetest tunes."

Meanwhile, back at Brooks —

Brooks felt a new presence within his walls and quickly recognized the soul called Len.

The entire Brooks estate was primed to inspire Len. The walls were charged and ready to project ideas and inspiration. The chandeliers stood ready to illuminate concepts. The floors had many years of experience directing intentions in an ascending motion. The four corners of every room knew they had special powers, and when they united, those powers would merge to form a single body of thought that hopefully Len would understand.

The sensory stations in the forest were ripe and ready to inspire those seeking insight. When those sensory stations were unitedly activated, their concentrated powers were magical.

Len had been a shadow presence for a very short time and still had much to learn. He figured out quickly how to exchange ideas with other souls, and they had been immensely helpful in his orientation. Len had yet to find the courage to try an interchange with his beloved Dora and hoped to make that happen while in the space called Brooks. There was a certain anxiety about that interchange because he figured she must have questions only he could answer by now. He had important information for her, and he was trying to make progress in his orientation to this new existence, so he could assist her to move forward as a mortal.

22

Trust your gut, like a hound on a scent; It knows the way.

Whispered strains of Mozart's *Clarinet Concerto* played softly in the background while Dora worked, her mouth set in determination.

The music lasted about a half hour and was on a loop nearing the end of its third repeat. Len's eclectic taste in music had always been one of his most exciting eccentricities. He listened to jazz when he created a project at his workbench in the garage and found energy in rock and roll from the sixties when he cleaned and organized. His favorite country singers serenaded him as he tended to his yardwork, and neighbors often heard him singing along at the top of his lungs to gospel music. A few even caught him raising his arms in pleading appeal.

Len had particularly liked piano music. His favorite song was, "Love Is a Many Splendored Thing." He and Dora heard that song on their first date to a drive-in picture show. It was a story of love between a male American reporter and a Eurasian female doctor encountering prejudice from her family and Hong Kong society about their union. The movie ended with the reporter being killed in the war and the last words to his lover penned in a letter. He wrote her to remember the many splendored things they got to experience, which many people never do. It was filmed in 1955 and finally reached the drive-in theater, where cars filled with young people enjoyed a night out with friends, or young lovers imagined their love stories in the making.

Len and Dora were part of an irreverent foursome, all sixteen-year-olds, finding humor in the love scenes. They clumsily tried to deflect the awkwardness of those moments by overacting the scenes they witnessed. They were simply four young people out for a night of frivolous entertainment. They quickly found it via the speaker hanging in the open car window of an old jalopy on a warm summer's evening. The car was littered with popcorn, candy wrappers, and drinks precariously balanced as they acted out scenes interspersed with raucous laughter. This noise would not be tolerated in a regular movie theatre, but the drive-in was a different ballgame. As the years progressed, "Love Is a Many Splendored Thing" became an enchanting reminder of two young people discovering the beginnings of love for the first time.

A couple of years ago, their youngest daughter, Robyn, gave them a unique Christmas gift to help them relive the memory she had often heard as her parent's first date. She gave them a DVD of the movie, a bag of buttered popcorn, a couple of bottles of Coke, and a big box of Milk Duds to share. Dora smiled sadly at the remembrance.

When Len wanted to concentrate without distractions, he played light classical music, like the one Dora listened to today. The music officiated the unraveling of her finances.

She let out a deep-seated sigh as she leaned back in the chair and released the vice-grip she had on her pencil. Within the pages of her notebook was a testament to the problem, she thought it might be manageable, at least for a short time, while she sought a permanent solution.

Fortunately, the mortgage on her family home was not as hefty as she thought. She should be able to pay it off with insurance money even after the loan on the policy was satisfied. Len's 401K account had a loan against it, and that would have to be satisfied at some point, but it wasn't anything she needed to worry about right away. The account would stay safe and lend security for later years.

The maxed out credit cards were a priority and more of an immediate problem. The recent purchases were for building materials Len likely used for Brooks. He and Roger had also done some much-needed upkeep on the family home she occupied. The cards had zero percent interest rates for six-month periods, which was a pleasant surprise for Dora. Initially, she had assumed interest rates in the twenty-percentile range, but these cards offered special incentives for new accounts. She noted that she had about four months to get the problem under control.

Fortunately, Brooks was free and clear, but part of the debt appeared to be a settlement of back taxes when the title was transferred to Len in probate. There were also some sizable legal fees associated with that transaction.

On the plus side, Dora had a small savings account. Aunt Becca had passed and left her with what she called an "Oh $h*t Stash" slush fund. Dora laughed, remembering the stories about her aunt's colorful vocabulary. Those tales recounted through the years by Eva regaled the adventures of her mother and Aunt Becca. They used to joke that they had been womb mates because they were twins. Growing up, they were best friends and constant companions.

Aunt Becca and Uncle Charlie lived a wonderful, adventure-filled life due to Uncle Charlie's career as a diplomat in public service. They had one child, a girl, who died in a tragic accident as a toddler. That event changed Aunt Becca. Her grief hung on her like a shroud for the next thirty years, and when Uncle Charlie died, Aunt Becca became a recluse living only a few months longer. She left Dora a few dollars and instructions to do something that would make her life exciting and fun. She hadn't touched the money, hoping to use it someday to finance a second honeymoon for her and Len.

Dora got up from the office chair and stretched the kinks out of her back. The sag in her shoulders lifted as she realized she could now concentrate on solving the mystery of the box she and Jean had discovered earlier.

The concerto started another loop of Mozart, and Dora stopped its progression. She returned to the box in the kitchen for a more thorough inspection. She found a large envelope of pictures taken of the house during its construction phase and set them aside to be part of her Brooks History wall.

She also found a small diary with notes from the first Grant family to live in Brooks. There were birthdates and other milestones likely made by Beth Grant. Dora made a note to make a shadow box with the picture of Beth and Timothy, making it a focal point of the history wall. She picked up the small envelope from the Mondale Bank holding the key and decided it belonged to the safety deposit box Len told her about. She made a mental note to go to the bank and sign the signature card.

Right now, she wanted to go back to Brooks. She knew Jean would have loved to be there, but for some reason, she felt the need to do this alone. So, with a notebook in hand, she made the trek to Brooks. The car's radio was tuned to an oldies station, and Dora hummed along to "Summer Place," one of her favorites. She smiled, remembering her junior prom and how she and Len had glided across the gym floor. Len was a good dancer, and all her friends told her how dreamy they looked dancing to that song. So many years ago, dances, and dreams ago.

The song ended as she pulled up to the front of Brooks.

Dora grabbed her bag, exited the car, and headed to the front door. The key on the long yellow cord was clutched in her hand, and the "Welcome to Brooks – Come on In" doormat seemed to welcome her. She felt a slight tingle as she used the key to open the front door.

She started up the staircase and grasped the railing, ascending each stair as her hand slid upward, barely dusting the surface. Dora was tall, not thin, but nicely curved, and carried herself well. She didn't know she was beautiful. When people met Dora, the first thing they noticed was her smile. It was inviting, warm, and genuine. She never came across as vain and was most comfortable in casual clothes. She didn't wear much makeup and preferred to secure her naturally wavy hair streaked with gray in a claw clip. A few militant curls often found their way out of the clip and hung loosely down her neck and around her face.

Dora reached the top of the stairs, turned left, and was drawn to the room at the end of the hall, where the door was ajar. She nudged it fully open, stepped inside, and flipped the light switch, starting the ceiling fan. The focal point was the four-poster bed with a crepe canopy of gauze-like fabric hanging in delicate folds. The beautiful Starlight quilt and contrasting pillows covered the bed. The room had one east facing window. It was flanked by two oversized chaise-like chairs covered in tufted maroon upholstery fabric. It looked like the perfect place to immerse in a book on a rainy afternoon or welcome the sun rising over the mountain in the background. Reading lamps dutifully stood at the back of each chair, ready to do their part in the event the occupants wanted to read as the day surrendered to shadows of nightfall.

Dora instinctively walked to the chair on the right and lowered herself to the edge, then lifted her legs for a full recline. She put a small pillow behind her head and continued to survey the room. Two large chests of drawers stood against one wall. A small, mirrored dressing vanity complete with a chair on the opposite wall, and an enormous wardrobe beside it. The papered walls were covered with tiny multi-shades of pastel flowers.

Dora leaned her head back and studied the swirling pattern of the ceiling, that seemed to end where the chandelier was mounted. The blades of the fan rhythmically spun in the same swirling pattern. The light from the chandelier sparkled as it bounced off each piece of cut-glass prism. She closed her eyes, and her body settled into the chair. Her breathing took on a relaxed rhythm, and she fell asleep.

Unafraid, she skimmed the earth's surface at a mind-spinning pace and wondered where she would end up. As quickly as her journey started, it stopped. She was in the middle of a meadow with various shades of green and sitting on velvet soft grass. A perfectly formed tree offered shade from branches heavily laden with an unrecognizable fruit nestled amongst large dark green fronds of leaves. A gurgling creek accompanied a chorus of birds singing to the meadow and its wildlife. She sat with her eyes closed. She thought she might open her eyes and add the sense of mortal sight to this magical place but decided the picture in her head needed to be protected. She tightly clenched her eyes and smiled serenely.

Then, it happened.

It was not at all scary, and it seemed natural. Dora felt a softness near, a beautiful, reassuring presence, something like a whiff of air so close to her lips she wanted to take a deep, inhaling breath and hold it captive. She tried to open her arms and encircle the unknown presence, holding it to her chest where her heartbeat quickened. The presence lingered and then seemed to dissipate. With dogged determination, Dora tried to keep it close for a little longer. She knew if she was to release it, she may not be able to regain it.

With deliberate effort, Dora barely opened her eyes, then she widened them fully. Len stood before her with the sweetest little boy smile, bright, sparkling blue eyes, and that little tuft of a cowlick on the crown of his head.

"Len, is that you?"

Len started to speak, but nothing came out, and instead, he vanished like a cloud imploding in the wind.

Startled, she sat quiet for a time, then shook her head to clear the cobwebs that metaphorically clouded her brain. She closed her eyes again and concentrated, determined to bring Len back. If it was real, then he could reappear. If she were dreaming, then the dream would recommence. Either way, it was an experience she desperately wanted. Some might call it crazy, but more time with Len was worth the title because, for a moment, a heart-racing moment, he was real.

Dora lay on the chair for quite a while, but nothing happened, and she decided it was a dream, just a beautiful dream. She gathered her purse and left the room, retracing her steps back to her car and her life alone. She had intended to open the mailbox with the key she had found yesterday but remembered she had promised Jean the experience of solving that mystery. So, she left the discovery for another day. However, for some reason, she was more confident than ever that she was nearing a critical revelation.

23

Don't be too proud to ask for a hand;
We all need help from time to time.

Len was fully aware he was no longer a living, breathing mortal requiring oxygen. Why then was he left gasping for air he wasn't supposed to need?

How did this happen? He was not supposed to be able to be seen yet. He had not completed orientation and had been told it was hazardous to attempt that level of soulism without authorization. He would only be given permission when those in charge were certain he could handle it. He was puzzled.

He had seen Dora asleep on the chair, dozing and so incredibly beautiful. He went to her without restraint and leaned in, feeling the familiar intimacy he treasured. He tried to take in her perfume, the clean smell of her hair, the loveliness of her skin. This was all so hard, and he felt ungrateful once more for not fully appreciating the miracle of being mortal.

Len felt great relief as he sensed sweet Dora to be okay. He worried about her. He would love her forever, a determination he made many years ago when they married. When the minister pronounced those words of *till death do you part*, Len decided then and there that nothing would constrain his love for the girl staring into his eyes and pledging her love to him. She had been in his every thought, especially during the months before his untimely exit from life.

Since his passing, he often wished he had immediately presented her with his wonderful gift rather than waiting. Who knows how long it's going to take to figure this out?

Len's mortality had ended unexpectedly. He had not been sick and felt full of life when it suddenly stopped, and all his magnificent plans sat unfinished in a sphere where he didn't exist. Life was certainly unpredictable. Len chuckled as only a soul can do, *"Life—one day you're in, and the next day you're out."*

Len knew there was one mortal, a lawyer named Jake, who could solve the problem Len had left behind. Still, he didn't understand how to communicate with that person. Everything he had been taught in his new existence told him he was far from ready to try that feat.

Len knew Dora had made a little progress in discovering his secrets. Unfortunately, she had only gone as far as finding out about poor financial planning on his part, potentially the most damaging part of the plan. Len didn't want Dora to think badly of him. Throughout their marriage, he was her hero, her knight in shining armor. He wanted to move things along, so she got to the part where his hero status could be reclaimed. He wanted the two of them to lock eyes, share smiles, and see Dora wiggle her nose again as a sign they were still in love.

Len treasured those memories.

Because he had become adept at changing spaces, he transported himself to the gardens of Brooks. There, he felt at one with nature and could soak it in. Everything about the forest attested to the presence of a higher being, and Len absorbed that intelligence. Much of his orientation had come from places like this. When he was given a choice for private contemplation, he quickly selected Brooks.

He recalled the many distractions he endured in mortality. He now knew that the eternal nature of souls coexists with mortals in a very symbiotic fashion. He now understood that being a human is nothing short of incredible, a beautiful gift from the ultimate creator of the world and humanity.

24

*Count your blessings – It's like counting fireflies
on a summer night.*

Dora loved the quiet of the world in the early morning hours. She lingered beneath the covers, trying to recall a dream that now regularly insinuated itself in her slumber. Each time it appeared, she tried vainly to embrace it, but the delusion always vanished much too soon, leaving her feeling pleasantly fulfilled and smiling in its recollection. She sat on the edge of her bed, realizing it was the two-week anniversary of Len's passing. The moment was brief and replaced with melancholy.

She stepped into the shower greeted with hot water and aromatherapy, a pulsating barrage of water attacked her neck and shoulders. She audibly thanked Len once again for installing it months ago and remembered his spiel as he justified the expenditure. "It'll make a difference in the effectiveness of our shampoo and conditioner and will be better for our skin," he said with consummate authority.

Dora finished her shower, dressed for the day, applied a little makeup, and pulled her hair into a ponytail. She sat on Len's side of the bed and opened his bedside drawer where, undisturbed, lay the familiar notebook holding his private thoughts. She opened it. The pages were dated, some with no more than one or two words. She smiled, seeing her name on various pages encircled with a heart. She closed the book and clutched it briefly to her chest before returning it to the drawer.

Dora kept herself busy with household chores for the next few hours, waiting to make her phone calls. Just after the nine o'clock hour hit, her phone rang.

"Hello, Grant household."

"Good morning. Is this Mrs. Len Grant?"

"Yes, it is, whose calling?"

"Mrs. Grant, my name is Penelope Davis. I'm with the Karvelas Law Firm here in Mondale."

"Oh, yes, my son said you'd be calling. What can I do for you?"

"Mrs. Grant, may I offer my sincere condolences about your husband? I didn't know him well, but he's been in our office several times and seemed like a gentleman. I'm so sorry for your loss."

"Thank you, Ms. Davis. Yes, he was a gentleman. I don't understand, though. Are you calling about the probate thing because I thought that was all settled?"

"No, Mrs. Grant, it's another matter that indirectly affects your probate. I want to discuss it with you. We have been working with your husband on a matter that will benefit you financially. Unfortunately, we haven't completed it until now, and well, you know."

"Oh yes, of course. I'll be in town today. I have a list almost as long as my arm of things I need to get done, and I want to spend some time later at our Brooks house. I can plan on being in your office around 5 p.m. If that's too late, you're welcome to come out to the house, and we can talk there."

There was a pause.

"I can move some things around and meet you in the office. It shouldn't take long."

"Great, I'll see you then. Bye."

Dora hung up the phone. "Benefit you financially." The words put a pep in her step.

Penny Davis hung up with a black-hearted smile. She was seated at her boss's desk and lifted her feet to the desktop. She leaned back in his chair, lacing her fingers behind her head, daydreaming about beautiful clothes, expensive jewelry, a fancy apartment, a costly automobile, and sunny beaches. She nearly tipped over when the ringing telephone interrupted her thoughts.

Penny grabbed the edge of the desk to right herself and pulled the chair close enough to get the receiver in hand. Just as she was going to press the button to connect the call, something told her she ought to let this one be answered with automation. She brought her hand back to the arm of the chair, listened to the invitation to leave a message, and then heard the familiar voice of her brother-in-law.

"Penny, it's Jake. You should be in the office. I'll try your cell. I need to talk to you about the Grant deal. If I don't get you on your cell, call me back. I've got a good SIM card now. This is important. Get back to me ASAP."

Penny waited a few minutes and then heard her cell phone ring in the adjoining office. She figured he would leave the same message. The clock was ticking, and her meeting this afternoon with Mrs. Grant was crucial. Penny used her time to organize Jake's desk so it would be presentable for her meeting with **her** important client later today.

Dora spent her day tending to errands and put a satisfying checkmark beside each item on her to-do list. Her last stop was the bank, where she instantly recognized Robyn's childhood friend, Myla Dawson.

"Mrs. Grant, how nice to see you. I'm so sorry about Mr. Grant. It seems unreal because he was here just a day or so before, and I spoke to him about Robyn, and we chatted. I was dumbfounded when I heard he had passed. I'm so very sorry. How are you doing? Can I get you some water or anything? I did get to see Robyn while she was home, and it was fun to catch up. Has she gone back to Australia? Her children are adorable. I loved listening to little Lenny talk, and my goodness, Rachel is a mini-Robyn. Oh, there I go, rambling all over the place. I'm sorry, what can I do for you today?"

Dora looked at the young woman and wondered how she could compose so many sentences without stopping for a breath. She remembered her son, Roger, being a mouthy teenager and asking Myla, "Don't you ever shut up?" Myla had laughed off the insult and continued her chatter.

"Thanks, Myla. I'm doing okay, and I'm getting used to a different life. I appreciate your kindness. I'm here because Len told me he had gotten a new safety deposit box, and I need to sign an updated signature card. I'd also like to look inside."

"Oh, yes, Mrs. Grant, I'll get it."

Myla pulled the card from the file cabinet, set it in front of Dora, and offered her a pen. Dora signed the card and pushed it back toward Myla.

"Do you have your key, Mrs. Grant?"

"Yes, I do." Dora pulled the small envelope from her purse and dumped the key into her hand.

They entered the vault, and Myla removed the box. She took it to a cubicle and set it on the table, then pulled out a chair and motioned to Dora.

"Thanks, Myla, I won't be long. I know it's getting close to quitting time."

"Take your time, Mrs. Grant. It always takes a few minutes for us to close out." She smiled and left the vault.

Dora opened the box and found all the usual papers neatly stacked, but at the bottom, there was a large manila envelope she didn't recognize. She tugged it loose, undid the metal clasp, and removed the contents.

At the top she read *Bearer Bonds,* then she scanned chunks of legal mumbo jumbo. She reasoned that the documents must have been important, or Len wouldn't have secured them this way.

Using her phone, she took a photo of the top bond and then put everything back. When she got back home tonight, she would review Len's notebook to see if he had written anything about them, and then call Roger to see what he knew. She checked her watch. It was almost time for her appointment with Ms. Davis. She stepped to the entry of the vault.

"Myla, I'm finished. Could you help me put this back, please?"

"Of course, Mrs. Grant."

"Please give your family my regards. Your mom sent over a casserole my family enjoyed. And I believe I saw a floral tribute from your parents. I promise to get out a proper thank you card."

"You're welcome. There's no hurry with those cards, Mrs. Grant. People will understand. Take your time and let us know if there's anything we can do to help."

Dora could tell that Myla was winding up again, so she waved good-bye and hurried out the door.

The law office was several blocks away, and Dora quickly found a parking spot. The office was on the third floor, with the elevator opening directly into the reception area. No one was at the desk, but a woman appeared in the doorway of the adjoining office. She smiled and extended her hand.

"Mrs. Grant, I assume. I'm Penelope Davis. I'm glad to see you. I'll lock off this elevator door, so we won't be disturbed. I don't have any other appointments, and my secretary has left for the day." Penny nodded toward the reception desk.

"Of course. I'm looking forward to hearing what you have to tell me. Len always took care of the business side of our marriage. I don't have any idea what this is about."

"Well, come into my office, and we'll discuss it. I must apologize for the clutter. I've been so busy. My secretary is a good administrator, but she knows nothing about the complexities of law. I need to hire a paralegal. Have a seat, Mrs. Grant. Can I get you anything, a water or soda? Perhaps you'd like a snack?"

"I'd love some water, nothing to eat, though."

"Give me a minute. I usually have my secretary here to do these things. She's so good to help make my clients feel at ease."

Penny left and returned with a cold Evian. She handed it to Dora along with a napkin.

Dora took a long gulp and dabbed her mouth with the napkin. "Oh, that is so good. I didn't realize how thirsty I was. Thanks, it hit the spot."

"That's fine. Let me know when you need another, I have them on ice. Mrs. Grant, your husband came to me two weeks ago and showed me a picture of a bearer bond he said he found in the attic of the Brooks house. I've spent this past week investigating the document and finally have an answer. I have some bad news and some good news. First of all, the documents in his possession are real. They were issued in 1925 by Pead

Semiconductors and probably secured with money from the people who owned the Brooks house. The thing about bearer bonds is that they are issued to no one in particular. They're owned by whoever possesses them. Through the years, this form of speculative investing has been done away with, and they are not issued anymore. The United States Government found that they were being used as an easy way to launder ill-gotten gain and disallowed them in the fifties."

Dora held up her hand, stopping Ms. Davis from continuing. "If that's the case, why am I here? I thought you said there could be a financial gain."

"I'm getting to that part. In some instances, the issuing companies have paid possessors a reward, in exchange for the bonds to get them out of circulation. The original issuer was bought out years ago by another company, and in good faith, the new owner is willing to pay you fifty-thousand dollars for the bonds. My office has spent about twenty hours on this matter, so there will be a fee. However, you'll still realize about forty-five thousand dollars for the deal. The company said they would cut the check and give it to you within twenty-four hours of surrendering the bonds. If you give me the bonds, I'll have them delivered by an insured courier service, and you could have your check this time tomorrow."

Dora sat for a few minutes, gathering her thoughts, and sipping the water. "Ms. Davis, I'm thankful for all of this. It's going to help my situation a great deal."

"Mrs. Grant, do you know where the bonds are now?"

"Well, I didn't until about a half hour ago. I've just come from the bank, where I had to sign a new signature card for a larger safety deposit box that Len secured before his passing. When I went through the contents, I found the documents inside. I have a picture of one of them on my phone."

Penny felt a chill rush through her body, and two and one-half million goosebumps popped up on her arms and shoulders when she heard that this woman had touched the bonds within minutes of her arrival at the office. It was all Penny could do to maintain her composure as Dora continued.

Dora pulled out her phone, brought up the picture, and handed it to Ms. Davis.

"Oh yes, that's it. Your husband showed me a similar picture on his phone. It's how I was able to identify the issuing entity. Mrs. Grant, can you return to the bank and get that envelope? I'll wait for you, and we'll get this started immediately."

"They were closing when I left, and Monday is a holiday, so I won't be able to get them before Tuesday. Besides that, I'd like to discuss this with my son. It's all so new to me."

"Of course, I want you to feel comfortable with all this. But remember, this company doesn't have to give you anything for the bonds. You can keep them and use them to start a fire in one of those fireplaces at Grandpa's house if you want to. They're worthless. I took the liberty of telling the company about the loss of your husband, and they feel a sense of altruism to help out. I wouldn't wait too long to follow through. The sooner you have that money, the better for you."

"Yes, of course, but my hands are tied until Tuesday anyway. I'll get back to you."

Dora arose from her chair and left the office. She stepped into the elevator and watched as the door closed and Ms. Davis was no longer in view. Dora knew that a windfall of this magnitude would solve her financial problems, but something seemed off, and being patient seemed the most prudent thing to do.

Penny was like a predator in hot pursuit as she followed the woman to the elevator. She unlocked the elevator door and then watched Dora step into the space and push the button. Penny stared with frustration as the position indicator for the elevator lit up showing Dora's descent. She glanced at the reception desk where she usually sat, and the blank spot where she had removed her nameplate. She angrily stomped her foot. Penny didn't want anyone else getting involved in this matter. She didn't know the son, but she was sure his influence wouldn't be helpful to her cause, and what's with those stupid Monday holidays?

Her best hope had been that Dora would be as anxious as she was to get this issue resolved. The fewer people involved, the better. Aside from all that, Jake had called again and left messages on both phones. He couldn't be put off much longer without raising suspicion.

25

There's always something to learn—
Stay as curious as a cat in a barn.

Dora got to her car and placed a call to her son but got his voice mail. He was probably still at the hardware store, and she didn't want to bother him there, so she left a message that she would call later. Her phone rang while she was mulling over the meeting with Ms. Davis, and according to the caller ID, it was Jean, who always seemed to know when Dora needed a friend.

"Hi, Jean, I was just thinking of calling you."

"Something told me I needed to call you, my friend. How are you?"

"Well, right now, I'm feeling a little discombobulated."

"That's a word I haven't heard in a long time. What's the cause of your discombobulation, and how can I help?"

"I'm on my way to Brooks. I want to take a few pictures of the sunset and evening shadows for a brochure Roger is designing for me. Something happened today, and I need to talk to someone about it. Are you available?"

"Sure, I'd love to go back out there. I'll leave in about fifteen minutes and meet you."

"Great. Hey, you bought lunch the last time. Are you in the mood for another meal from Kravers?"

"Absolutely, the usual, please."

"I'll pick it up."

A half hour later, Dora pulled into the Brooks' driveway and was greeted with the smiling face of her friend sitting on the doorstep. She pulled up alongside Jean's car, turned off the engine, and climbed out of the car.

"Sorry, I hope you haven't been waiting too long."

"Nonsense, this place is like a little piece of heaven. I feel so serene out here. I've been enjoying the quiet. I could almost feel the strength of having a big brother watching over me."

"Let's go inside. I have much to tell you."

Dora unlocked the door and the two went inside.

"Let's eat in the kitchen at the breakfast nook. It gives us a great view of the gardens."

Dora set the lunch sack and cup holder on the counter and Jean took a seat.

"I'm hungry, it looks and smells divine," said Jean. "I took the day off from work to clean out my basement. I would probably have eaten a cold pizza and fallen asleep in front of the TV."

Jean picked up the puffy bag of chips and pulled it at the sides. The bag responded with an explosive puff, shooting chips hither and yon.

"And that is how not to open a bag of chips. I don't suppose you want me to help you with your bag, do you?

Dora laughed and opened her chips without collateral damage, sending both women into fits of laughter.

"Here, have some of mine. I've had a busy day, too, and I got everything accomplished on my list. Now, I can finally start concentrating on getting this place up and running."

The two women enjoyed their food for a few minutes before Dora broke the silence.

"Jean, something happened today, and I need some advice."

"Okay, what happened?"

"I got a call from a lawyer, Penelope Davis. She's with the Karvelas Law Firm in town, and Len was working with them before he died. Len found some old documents here at Brooks and wanted help identifying them."

The floorboards shifted beneath their feet and an inaudible whisper moved through the electrical wiring, but the women were unaware.

"Remember the box we discovered near the front door? Len had left it there and meant to bring it home but forgot it, and then you and I went through it a few days ago."

"Yeah, go on."

"A few days before his passing, he asked me to go to the bank and sign a new signature card for a bigger safety deposit box he had secured. I did that today, and I found the envelope containing the documents. Look, let me show you."

Dora pulled up the picture she had taken with her phone and showed it to Jean.

"Oh, wow."

"Well, this lawyer found out the bonds are worthless these days, though they were once quite valuable. The government outlawed this form of investment back in the 1950s. The bonds belong to whoever has possession, and as they are recovered, there are instances where the finder is awarded a recovery fee. Supposedly, the present company that bought the original one is willing to give me a reward of fifty thousand dollars for turning them in. After paying legal fees, I would get about forty-five thousand."

Jean's eyes widened, and her eyebrows shot up.

"You always land on your feet, Dora, you're like a cat with nine lives. This is wonderful news, and I'm thrilled for you."

"I feel like I'm waiting for the other shoe to drop. It seems too good to be true." She paused, "But I left the meeting with a strange discomfort and even doubt."

"It does sound a little bit like a fairy tale ending. But, hey, be grateful. Somebody up there likes you." Jean pointed to the heavens.

A covert presence stood outside the kitchen entry and listened. Brooks had summoned this presence, and he strained to hear the voice of his beloved. He wanted to burst onto the scene and tell her what he knew. Somehow, he had to warn her, but at this point, he wasn't allowed to reveal himself outside the walls of Brooks and not in the presence of the general public.

"Do you think it's legit, Jean? Should I go ahead and turn over the documents to this woman? She said I would have payment within twenty-four hours of the company getting them. She said she would use a private courier service, and I would be paid quickly."

"Sure, but make sure you get the money first. Only give up the documents if there are dollars to hand over. I know the woman is a lawyer and everything, but money does strange things to people. She could take the bonds, get the reward, and never see you again. Maybe you ought to check her credentials."

"I agree, Jean. I need to have a higher level of trust. The thing is the company will only pay if they have the bonds in hand. Besides, I was there, it's a law office. I've seen it in town, and I've seen it advertised for years. I don't know her, but the office is real."

"Why didn't you use that office for the probate?"

"We didn't have any choice in that matter. It was all handled by Len's grandfather's lawyer, and that office was located in the city where Granddad lived."

"Well, if you're sure of the law office and have money in hand, I say go for it."

"Yeah, that sounds reasonable."

The pair finished their sandwiches while exchanging small talk, and then they gathered and disposed of the errant chips and trash.

"Well, as my dad would have said, daylights a burnin', and I see the beginnings of a beautiful sunset."

26

Treat folks with kindness, like you would your kinfolk.

THE FOLLOWING DAY, Dora had two messages on her phone. The first was from Ms. Davis at the law office, and the second was from Roger. He told her he would try calling again during his lunch break in the afternoon. Dora didn't expect to hear from the lawyer before Monday as they had agreed, so she ignored the directions to call Ms. Davis back.

She was an optimistic sort of person but also slightly pragmatic. She never dwelled too long on things that were out of her control because there was nothing she could do about them. Rather, she spent her energy changing things within her power to revise and prayed for wisdom to make a good decision. Through the years, some accused her of being unrealistic. Still, Dora's objective about situations had always been to solve problems by planning for positive and negative outcomes. In her observations, too many people looked on the dark side, dwelling on negativity, thus not recognizing positive solutions that might otherwise be obvious. She felt that being happy was closely associated with staying busy and involved in life's experiences and being of service to others.

Dora had been taught to follow the teachings of Christ, and she lived by parables in the New Testament. She particularly loved the Sermon on the Mount, where Christ taught the Beatitudes, and she genuinely appreciated the diversity of humanity. Through the years, Dora often learned valuable life lessons from those not in her immediate sphere of influence. Enlightened experiences were added to her cache as that group of people widened.

Strangely, she felt optimistic about her current circumstances and was confident that life would work out. She also felt herself drawn to Brooks. Somehow, she recognized a kinship to the house, where she could feel a trusted confidant's guidance and influence. She admitted being dubious toward Len when he rehearsed his affinity for the house. She felt his stance to be rather dramatic.

Dora gathered supplies for Brooks, including the key she hoped would fit the mailbox, but just as she walked out the door, the bell rang, and a young woman with a broad, welcoming smile stood holding a floral arrangement.

"Are you Dora Grant?"

"Yes, I am." Dora dug into her purse and handed the delivery girl a cash tip as she handed off the bouquet. The card accompanying it read, "Penelope Davis, Law Office." She put the arrangement on the dining room table and continued to her car, looking forward to spending some heart time in the country.

She pulled off the main road onto the graveled drive, passed the big old sugar maple tree, and rounded the bend. She stepped out of the car and breathed in the tranquility of the grounds, then lugged in the tote bags filled with supplies and deposited them near the door on the floor. She was still startled at how welcome she felt here.

Penny was fit to be tied. She called Dora this morning and had to leave a message asking her to call back. The bothersome widow hadn't, and the morning wore on. Penny had finally relented and taken a call from Jake. It took some fast talking to keep him from hopping on the first plane bound for home. As bad luck would have it, he had secured an internet connection. When he looked at the local paper online, he found the obituary for Len Grant. Jake told her to send flowers to Mrs. Grant with his condolences and that he would take care of the bond details when he got home at the end of the week. Penny promised to take care of everything, and now she was under the gun to put her plan in place in no less than forty-eight hours.

Dora worked throughout the morning and afternoon, organizing the kitchen at Brooks. It was busy work but kept her mind occupied. After going through Len's phone last night and discovering the phone number of Jake Karvelas, she had more questions than ever about the Karvelas Law Firm and where Penelope Davis fit with it all. Ironically, her phone bounced, vibrating on the tiled counter. She picked it up and checked the caller ID but didn't recognize the number. Nevertheless, she answered it.

"Hello."

"Hello, is this Dora Grant?" said a male voice.

"Yes, it is. What can I do for you?"

"Mrs. Grant, I'm Jake Karvelas from the Karvelas Law Office. I met your husband about a month ago and discussed a legal matter. I don't believe he told you anything about it, and I just found out about Len's passing. Please accept my deepest condolences to you and your family. Mrs. Grant, I need to talk to you."

"I only found out about my husband's dealings with you from the lawyer at your office a few days ago. I'm working with that lawyer now to close the matter out."

"You say you're working with a lawyer from the Karvelas Law Office? Who is that?"

"It's Ms. Davis. She's having me surrender the bonds to get my reward. She said I would get about forty-five thousand after legal fees to get them out of circulation. She just left another message on my phone. I have yet to call her back."

"Mrs. Grant, please wait to do anything until I get there. I'm in Greece now, but I'll catch a flight and get back as quickly as possible. The Karvelas Law Office is my firm."

"The bonds are in the bank in our safety deposit box, and I can't get to them before Tuesday anyway because of the holiday on Monday. I told her all of that when we talked. I don't know why she's calling me again."

"Just wait for me, I'd rather handle this myself. In the meantime, keep your bonds securely locked up."

"Of course, but what do I tell Ms. Davis?"

"Call her, but don't tell her you've talked to me. That's important. Arrange to meet her in a couple of days. I'll get there and take care of everything else but leave your bonds in the bank."

"Okay, I'll set up a meeting at Brooks for Tuesday afternoon. Do you think that will work for you?"

"Yes, that should be fine, and I know where Brooks is, Mrs. Grant. I've always admired it. Let's plan on meeting there at 4 p.m. on Tuesday."

"Okay. My mother's activity group will be at the house, but we can meet in the library. It's quiet and closed off. I'll look forward to seeing you, Mr. Karvelas."

"Mrs. Grant, your husband was a good man, and he was trying to settle this matter so the two of you could enjoy a retirement of service to others. I want to help you fulfill that purpose. I'll explain more as soon as I get back. I've already called the clearing house I've been working with and updated them about the situation. Do not surrender those documents to anyone."

"I won't, Mr. Karvelas. Thanks for your call."

Dora's curiosity ran rampant. She had so many questions. Since Jean loved mysteries, perhaps she could help with this one. A phone call got the ball rolling, and without much convincing, Jean jumped at the chance to be a detective.

"I'll be in the kitchen, and the front door is unlocked."

An hour later, Jean strode through Brooks' front door and followed the clanging of cans she heard from the kitchen.

"You must plan on feeding an army."

"Hi, yeah, I'm stocking up. Come help me empty these boxes."

"Okey, dokey. So, tell me what you need, boss lady."

Dora turned to her friend and narrowed her eyes. "Jean, how would you like to help me solve a mystery?"

"I'd love it. What are we going to do?"

"I need you to do some minor detective work for me. It's about the lawyer I told you about, Penelope Davis from the Karvelas Law Firm. I spoke with Jake Karvelas from that firm by phone a little bit ago. He wouldn't explain much, but we've scheduled a Tuesday afternoon meeting at Brooks. Further, he told me not to say anything to Ms. Davis about him calling me but to go ahead and arrange with her to meet here as well. This

Jake guy seems genuine, but I feel uneasy about this and want to be prepared. I think you can help ease my mind."

"Go ahead, spell it out."

"Remember our conversation the other day about the bonds and the reward, yada, yada, yada?"

"I remember?"

"Ms. Davis is pushing me to turn the bonds over to her so she can get the check for me, and now Mr. Karvelas has told me to wait for him to get here."

"That is interesting."

"I'm curious why Mr. Karvelas is so mysterious about not making his presence known to the woman associated with his firm. I don't know. I'm not normally suspicious, but I'm skittish on this one for some reason. My common sense is telling me to be wary."

"Okay, I trust your cautious side. Besides, I've always wanted to be a PI. I've been watching reruns of *Perry Mason,* and my favorite character is Paul Drake. He is one sexy-looking dude. Who was your favorite character on that show?"

Dora took a little time to answer.

"It's funny. Back then, my favorite was Della. She wore classy clothes and worked in a fancy office for an important man in the big city. She was brainy and never got rattled. I took type and shorthand classes in high school, and I figured being Della Street was something I could do. What I should have been thinking was to go to law school and be an attorney in the big city, where I would hire a secretary and a private investigator who looked like Paul Drake. I don't know why I didn't have bigger aspirations than being a secretary." Dora shook her head at the reminder of her youthful, unambitious nature. "Let's get back to the subject. You want to be my Paul Drake?"

Jean's demeanor got visibly brighter.

"I'll change my name to Paula Drake and get a little notebook, but I refuse to take up smoking again. I got that demon off my back many years ago, and I'm not falling under his spell again." Jean finished with a decisive nod as she put the last can of diced tomatoes on the shelf. She gathered the empty boxes. "I'll take these to the recycle bin."

Jean came back in, and Dora pulled a folded paper from her apron pocket.

"Great. I've written down names and phone numbers for you. Just do a little digging for me and let me know what you come up with. I'm hopeful you can verify the Karvelas Law Office's veracity and who the owner is. I'm curious whether this Ms. Davis is genuine and has a good reputation around town for being honest."

"Well, my second husband had some dealings with that law office years ago, but it wasn't a woman he worked with. It was a guy, and George thought he was a good lawyer."

"Jean, I've known you for at least thirty years, and I know you've only had one husband, and his name wasn't George. What are you talking about?"

"Hey, I'm trying to create an air of mystery about me, Dora. Paul Drake had this mysterious side, you know. He had a *devil may care* look in his eye, and I don't think he carried a gun, yet he walked around like he could take care of business when he had to. When I get a gun, I'll wear it in one of those shoulder harnesses and get a great jacket to conceal it."

Dora laughed. "Jean, *please* don't get a gun. Honestly, don't go overboard with this. I need you to check out this woman's credentials and those of the office. I don't want to worry about you shooting yourself in the foot."

"You're a killjoy. I'd look so cool with a gun and a notebook on a stakeout waiting for Ms. Davis to make her next crafty move."

"You are nutty, and I'm ready to go home, but before you leave, let's see if we can solve one of our mysteries with this little key."

Dora pulled out the small key with a filigree pattern on a leather fob, and Jean followed her to the mailbox sitting on the counter. It fit perfectly, and Dora reached in and pulled out a handful of mail. It was all addressed to Recipient, Box 55B RFD 1. She rifled through it and realized it was junk mail. She also pulled out a small bag secured with a drawstring. Inside it, there was paper money and a few coins. When she looked at it closer, she realized it was Mexican money.

"Oh my gosh, would you look at this? That's a funny thing to put inside a mailbox."

Dora separated the coins and stacked the bills.

"Well, this is interesting," said Jean. "Do you know anything about Mexican money?"

"No, not at all."

"Yeah, it would be interesting to know how, when, and why it all ended up in the mailbox."

Dora stuffed the money in the pouch and held it by the string handle.

"Do you want to see a movie and go to dinner, my treat? There's a new Mexican place in town. Maybe they take pesos."

27

Holding grudges is like dragging a load of stone—
Forgive and forget.

Dora called the Karvelas Law Office the following day, and Ms. Davis answered with the first ring.

"Good morning, Ms. Davis, it's Dora Grant. Could you meet me at Brooks this afternoon at four?"

"Oh, Mrs. Grant. I assumed you'd bring the bonds to the office."

"Sorry, I'm just so busy and already at Brooks. If you could come here, it would be so helpful. I don't mean to be a problem."

"Well, okay, I'll be there at four."

"Great, thanks. I appreciate your flexibility. See you then."

Penny disconnected the call with a sigh of relief. She was glad to finally hear from the Grant woman and even more excited knowing that the whole thing would be in the bag by the end of the day. Her heart thumped with the idea of returning to Brooks, but at least it would be the last time she had to go there.

Within minutes, Dora's phone rang, and she was relieved to see it was a call from Jean.

"Morning, Jean, do you have anything for me?"

"Hi, Dora, where are you?"

"I'm at Brooks."

"I need to see you, Dora. I've got a lot of news, but I want to see your face when I tell you what I've found. I'll be there in a jiff."

"Okay, drive safe."

"Will do. I'm stoked, Dora."

Twenty minutes later, Jean dashed through Brooks' front door. She went to the kitchen and saw Dora standing on the countertop, rearranging dishes.

"Hey, Rapunzel, let down your hair."

Dora looked down at Jean and laughed at the image of her climbing a tower.

"Would you move that step stool this way, and I'll come down to you."

"Don't you know better than to be that far off the ground? What if you fell?"

Jean scooted the step stool closer for Dora to reach.

"You're right, I know better."

Jean gave Dora a warning glare.

"Let's sit at the breakfast nook. You said your mom and her group were coming over for a meeting. What time is that happening?"

"In about an hour. We've got time before things get rowdy."

"Dora, just wait till you hear what I've found. This has been so much fun. I'm made for this kind of work. This could be my new life. People talk about having a passion, and I've always wondered what that would be like. I've been digging into the past and uncovering stuff people would rather have stayed hidden. I'm excited to tell you about your Ms. Davis."

Jean stopped as abruptly as she began and stared at Dora's questioning face.

"Well, go ahead, I want to hear it all. What did you find out?"

Jean ceremoniously withdrew a small black notebook and thumbed a few pages into the book with quiet deliberation.

"The Karvelas Law Firm is legit and has been in business for almost twenty years. Its owner is Jake Karvelas, the only attorney in the office, and he has an impeccable reputation. Heads up, he has one other person in the office who looks after the administrative work, Ms. Penelope Davis, who is not a lawyer. My source tells me that Mr. Karvelas hasn't been seen for weeks. I thought that maybe Davis had murdered him and buried him somewhere. I got all excited about solving a killing. But you said a guy had called you and identified himself as Jake Karvelas. Darn it, I wanted to solve a murder case."

Dora rolled her eyes at her friend's dramatic discourse. "Then I was right to be suspicious. What do you think this Penelope person has in mind?"

"Wait, there's more." Jean flipped a page and went on.

"I decided to check her out a little deeper. She lives in the same house as Mr. Karvelas, which made my head spin, thinking there was some hanky-panky going on. It turns out she is the sister of Karvelas' wife, and she lives in the basement apartment of that home. It gets even more interesting, Dora. Ms. Penelope Davis got into trouble with her last job. She worked for an architectural firm as an admin, and it seems she got mixed up in a scheme to defraud her employer for a sizeable amount. She got caught in an audit, and they summarily dismissed her but didn't press charges. I'm guessing her sister conned the hubs into giving little sis work with limited privileges."

"Well, I'll be. That brazen female was going to con me, huh? She must have known those bonds were worth something to offer me fifty thousand. Wonder where she was going to get that kind of reward money?"

Dora thought for a couple of minutes while Jean looked on, and then she snapped her fingers.

"Actually," said Dora, "she said that she would take the bonds, get the money from the source, take out the fee for the law office, and bring me a check. She claimed she would have it done within a twenty-four-hour period. She probably never intended to get back to me with any money."

"What are you going to do, Dora? Let me help."

"I need to think about this. The bonds are locked away, and I'll keep them that way until I figure this out. I'm looking forward to meeting Mr. Karvelas."

"Dora, let's synchronize our watches."

"Really, Jean?"

28

Forgiveness is a gift you give yourself.

Penny parked her car in Brooks' driveway, took a deep breath, grabbed her fancy leather briefcase with the repaired strap, and draped it from her shoulder. A few cars were in the parking lot, and a van labeled *Mondale Assisted Living Center*. She took comfort in knowing there were other people on-site. Somehow, that gave her a sense of safety. She certainly wasn't afraid of Dora Grant, but the whole vibe of the house put her on edge. She silently reminded herself it was just an old house on a piece of dirt.

She stood to the side of her car and leaned against it momentarily as though she could drain the two-and-a-half-ton vehicle of strength. Instead, the car seemed to quiver.

Just as Penny pulled herself away and stepped toward the house, she heard something growl. She stopped, grabbed the bulk of her briefcase, wrapped it with both arms, and clutched it to her chest. She slowly turned, fully expecting to see a dreadful animal of some sort ready to pounce. There was nothing there. Her racing heart quieted, and she took a few deep, calming breaths.

She wished she had insisted that the meeting be in Jake's office. And, for at least the tenth time, she scolded herself out loud.

"Penny, stop being a skittery little rabbit."

About that time, she was startled as she spied a rabbit scurrying across the lawn and into the woods.

"Oh, for Pete's sake, this is ridiculous," she exclaimed.

Penny resolutely placed the briefcase strap on her shoulder again and practically marched to the front door like a soldier called to battle. She paused, wondering if the short in the bell had been fixed, then saw the metal plate at eye level on the door, "Welcome to Brooks – Come on In." She stepped carefully onto the doormat and, with some trepidation, slowly turned the door handle. At the same time, the door opened with some force behind it. A tiny woman sporting a smile was standing before Penny.

"Hi there, come on in."

"Uh, hello, my name is Penelope Davis. I'm here to see Dora Grant. She's expecting me."

"Yeah, she saw you pull up and ask me to let you in. I didn't mean to startle you. I'm Eva, Dora's mother. My friends and I came to have a get-together. You're welcome to join us. You're getting old, just like us, you know. That Botox stuff your generation uses doesn't fool anyone. I'll go get Dora."

Penny watched the diminutive-looking woman walk away and wondered at what age old people decided to dress outrageously and say whatever popped into their heads? When did they lose their filter about being politically correct and discreet? Had Eva not been an "old woman," Penny would have responded with a cutting remark. Instead, she took in her surroundings. At least a couple dozen old folks were milling around. It would appear, she guessed, that not one of them was under the age of eighty. Music from the rock and roll era played louder than necessary, and the women outnumbered the half-dozen men in the group. Some depended on canes to meander the room, while others pushed through groups using a walker; many decorated with all kinds of doodads, and it appeared that most people had dressed in the dark based on the color combinations she saw.

The women's caked-on makeup was haphazardly applied. Their crimson lipstick was defined in the wrinkles of their lips. The woman, Eva, had the most lavender hair Penny had ever seen, and sparkly fairy dust glimmered through shards of light as she moved. Embellishment was an understatement in describing the tortoiseshell frames of Eva's eyeglasses, which were much too big for her tiny face. Penny Davis continued to mentally critique the old woman wearing comfortable shoes, bedazzled jeans, and a tangerine-colored T-shirt emblazoned with the words *I'm not old* on the front and *I'm chronologically gifted* on the back. Penny decided that this woman was not only self-confident, but she also had a sense of humor.

"Ms. Davis, welcome to Brooks."

Penny turned at the sound of Dora Grant's voice. Dora wore a pair of bib overalls and a shirt, and her hair was covered with a scarf knotted at the back of her neck. Her face was smudged with rivulets of sweat. Dora pulled off her garden gloves as she approached her visitor.

"Hello, Mrs. Grant. You didn't say you were having a party when we made the appointment."

Dora wiped her hands down the front of her overalls.

"Oh, no, this isn't a party. You've met my mother. She lives at the Mondale Assisted Living Center and is their self-appointed Activities Director. She likes to bring her group over for their weekly planning meeting. Don't let their ages fool you. They can get rowdy and a little loud. Truthfully, they make me look forward to the aging process. Their motto is *you're only as old as you feel*," said Dora over the "Alley Oop" song currently blaring.

"Yeah, I guess so. Is there someplace we can go for privacy?" asked Penny.

"Of course, we can go into the library. I'll close the door to stifle the noise."

Penny didn't like the library, but she knew she must focus on getting her hands on the bonds and getting out of this place. She followed her hostess into the foreboding-looking room and waited by the entry while Dora closed the double doors. Penny stared at the bookcase behind the desk, wondering if a book would fly off the shelf aimed at her skull. She fixed her eyes on the face of a portrait hanging prominently on the wall, butting against the bookshelves, she waited for the eyes to blink or even go black.

She looked up at the immense chandelier and stepped to one side, worried that it might come spiraling down upon her. She quickly remembered the rocking chair in the alcove to her left and expected to see some movement. *Of course not, they're just inanimate objects.* She rebuked herself, then calmed when she heard her name.

"Ms. Davis, are you okay? Ms. Davis!"

"Oh, yes, I'm sorry. I got distracted for a moment. I'm fine. Do you have the bonds?"

"No, they're in our safety deposit box at the bank."

Penny was confused and then angry.

"I have other appointments, Mrs. Grant. It would be best if you had them here so we can finish this today. I don't have time to spare."

The arrogant tone broke, and her voice crackled with the last few words.

Dora walked around the room, stopping to admire a sculpture as she spoke with her back turned.

"Of course. I realize you're a busy lawyer with an active clientele." Dora turned and looked without expression as she continued.

"I admire powerful women, Ms. Davis. I never went to college myself. I'm in awe of women who push themselves academically, who decide early on to be in charge of their destiny."

Dora continued her circular pattern of the room and said, "I married young. All I wanted was to have a doting husband and children."

Dora stopped and turned to look at Ms. Davis. "Are you married, Ms. Davis?"

Penny thought for a minute. Mrs. Grant seemed different somehow. Penny had pegged her as an easy mark, but now she wondered. She straightened her shoulders and willed herself to look powerful.

"No, I'm not. I guess I'm married to my job," Penny said with something short of a laugh.

Dora smiled and nodded. "My oldest daughter is a career woman. Before she graduated from college, she was investigating opportunities for the right job. Within weeks of graduation, she found it. She's been with the same company for almost ten years and makes a good living. She's smart, independent, and bent on doing her best job. Unfortunately, she doesn't have much time for family these days. But I keep hoping she'll find room for all of us."

Dora picked up a small figurine from the bookshelf. "Do you have a family, Ms. Davis?"

"I have a sister. She's married and has children. I do holidays with them."

Dora replaced the statuette and remarked, "That's nice. Where did you graduate law school, Ms. Davis?"

Dora's tone had changed.

Penny felt she was not asking questions to be friendly. Her probing was meant to disarm.

She felt a paralysis of her plan forming. "Perhaps I should go. I have an appointment at the office, and I just remembered there are some things I need to do to be ready for it."

Penny put the briefcase strap across her shoulder and turned to the door only to find it opening with Eva's face peering around the corner.

"Dora, honey, your guest is here. Shall I bring him in?"

"Yes, Mother, please show him in."

Dora stood with a ringside seat to the biggest reveal of all times.

Penny's age-defiant face fell when Jake Karvelas strode through the door.

"Hello, Ms. Davis, how are things at the office?"

Penny looked like a live statue. She broke her stance when she mumbled, "Hello, Jake, how was your trip?"

Jake Karvelas' usual jovial manner had been replaced with one of sobriety, and each word was said with definition.

"It was good. My mother, Sarah, and the kids are still there. I came back a few days early. Would you be a good girl and go back to the office? I left you a note on your desk with some instructions. I expect to see those instructions carried out by the time I go in tomorrow morning. In the meantime, Mrs. Grant and I have some work to do."

"Yes, sir."

Penny walked past Jake and through the doorway. Somehow, the strap of her bag got hung up on the doorknob and jerked her backward. She took the strap off the doorknob, huffing in disgust. As she walked through the aged partygoers, an older man blocked her path.

"Hey there, you pretty little thing. How about I take you

home and show you my medicine cabinet," the old man said with a wicked glint.

"Get away from me," she snapped.

"Where have you been all my life?" said the old man, not easily deterred.

Penny stopped, turned, and said, "For the first half of it, I wasn't even born."

The older man laughed good-naturedly but seemed determined to get in the last word as he called out to her.

"Don't flatter yourself, missy. Remember, I'm retired and have plenty of time to pleeeese you."

"Dora, I need to apologize to you about Penelope Davis. She's my sister-in-law and has worked at my firm for several months. She takes care of my administrative work." He sighed and continued, "My wife is quite protective of her sister since only two are left in the family. Ms. Davis has made some poor choices, and though old enough to know better, she seems bent on finding an easy way rather than putting on work gloves and doing it right."

"That must be frustrating."

Jake nodded. "My wife and I gave her a port in the storm from her latest bad choice. I'm somewhat disappointed that she would take advantage of that kindness, and frankly, I don't know how to handle it."

Jake waited in silence for Dora's response.

"Mr. Karvelas, I don't blame you. Ms. Davis was quite convincing. But she didn't have me completely fooled. I've learned to trust my instincts throughout my lifetime, and something kept jabbing at me to be suspicious. I asked my friend to be an amateur sleuth, and she quickly came up with the facts you've just confirmed. I believe in second chances, and most of all, I trust my Len. I know he trusted you, and my instincts tell me I should, too."

Dora extended her hand to Jake Karvelas, and as he raised his face to hers, it was met with a full, honest smile. He clasped her hand with both of his, and they exchanged a contract of open hearts sealed with the signature of their grips.

"Thanks, Mrs. Grant. May I suggest we be on first-name terms?"

"Jake. Let me save you some time by telling you I spoke with my eldest daughter about these bearer bonds. She's a financial advisor of a major investment company, and she amply filled me in on all the technicalities and advised me on how to proceed. I've taken her first advice by securing a good attorney in you to handle the legalities. I'm ready to proceed."

"That's excellent news. I want you to feel completely comfortable in this whole transaction. I've spoken with the financial dignitaries of WJB Enterprises and set up a meeting to finalize the whole thing for a week from today. I want the two of us and even your daughter, if you like, to meet with Mr. Wilber Broadhead, the president. Dora, those bonds Len found in the attic of Brooks are worth more than two and a half million dollars. You, my good woman, are very wealthy."

Dora gasped. Hannah had told her she didn't know the exact value of the bonds, only that they were valid and probably worth a lot of money. Dora never expected anything of this magnitude.

"Oh, my goodness, I'm speechless. I've never dreamed of having anything close to that amount of money."

Jake chuckled. "We'll spend some time talking about investments and how to maximize them once we get the funds secured.

Many people will come out of the woodwork with hard luck stories to play on your generous nature. I hope you allow me to help you navigate that challenge and encourage you to lean on your daughter for investment advice. I liked your husband, Dora. He repeatedly told me how much he wanted to make your life comfortable. I've never known a man so absorbed in nature and the world and dedicated to helping humanity and ecology coexist. I've heard that couples start to resemble one another visually the longer they're together. I sense a resemblance in attitudes between you and Len, and it will do you well."

"Thanks, Jake. You and I will be a good team.

29

Honesty is the thread that weaves the fabric of trust in the tapestry of life.

As Penelope A. Davis drove back to the Karvelas Law Office, she didn't listen to the radio or talk to herself. She pulled into the office parking lot and saw a van marked *Mondale Lock and Key*. She went inside, and when she stepped out of the elevator, she found a man on his knees working on the disassembled door lock to Jake's office. He wore a worker's uniform likewise labeled.

"Who are you?" she asked.

"I'm changing the locks ma'am. Mr. Karvelas hired me."

The worker got up and faced the woman.

"Are you Ms. Davis?"

"Yes, I am."

"Mr. Karvelas said to expect you ma'am. He said the box on the desk is yours. There's a letter right there on the desk for you, too." He went back to his work.

Penny stepped closer to look inside the box. It had personal items she had accumulated and on top of it all was her nameplate,

Penelope A Davis, Paralegal. She picked it up, studied it for a moment, then dropped it into the trash can at the side of the desk. She hefted the box, turned on her heel, and reentered the elevator without a word to the worker. She pushed the button and went back to her car placing the box on the rear seat. With a sigh of dejection, she sat behind the wheel to read her fate.

Dear Penny:

This is something I don't enjoy, but Sarah and I have agreed it is necessary. You are no longer employed by our firm. Since you were not successful in defrauding my client, I will not be bringing charges against you for that attempt, or for false impersonation. However, you need to know that the Statute of Limitations gives me five years to change my mind. I have documented everything you have done, and I don't recommend you using my name or office as a reference. I will be truthful to anyone who asks for a reason for your dismissal. You will not be eligible for unemployment compensation.

You may continue to live in the basement of mine and Sarah's home, and you'll always be welcome at our table. Also, I will continue to pay for your health insurance. I suggest you use your time for the next few weeks to seriously reflect on your life choices and start looking at the Help Wanted ads for entry level positions.

Good luck, Penny. You may not believe it, but the children, Sarah, and I, do love you.

– Jake

30

Chase your dreams with grit and gumption;
They're yours for the taking.

It had been six months since Len Grant died, and there was a bittersweet party at Brooks since it was also the anniversary of the engagement of Len and Dora Grant. Brooks was a hub of activity, and everything about its five acres of plant, animal, and human life swelled with movement. A few people milled around the foyer, happily conversing as they pointed out different features of the house, their voices accompanied by soft strains of background music. There was also an extensive buffet table with a stack of plates, silverware, and paper napkins on one end, and an impressive spread of finger foods and several urns of assorted beverages.

Dora's casual attire was replaced with a lovely summer dress and strappy sandals. Her long gray hair swayed in shoulder-length waves.

"Jean, everything looks fantastic. Thank you so much for helping me put this together. You should have been an event planner."

"Just enjoy yourself. After I retired, I used my time planning this. It's been fun, but it's not something I'd want to do to make a living. That would turn into serious labor."

A new guest had arrived at the party and seemed enchanted by the mailbox. Dora took a minute to study her and then posed a question to Jean.

"Do you recognize the young woman who seems so fascinated by our little mailbox?"

Jean turned in the direction Dora nodded toward.

"No, I don't think I've ever seen her."

"I think I'll go introduce myself."

Jean said, "Okay, Dora, before you go, I need to talk to you about something. Could we meet in a little bit? Eva, Old Abe, and I have a proposition for you."

"Oh, oh, that sounds serious."

"Well, it is, but in a good way. It's nothing against the law."

Dora laughed. "Sure. Let's meet in the library in a half hour."

"Okay, I'll let the others know. In the meantime, I need to check the buffet table."

Dora walked to where the young woman stood, looking at the mailbox from different angles. She appeared to be in her twenties, her long, red hair with inevitable natural ringlets framing a sweetheart-shaped face. Her figure was that of an athlete, and when she looked toward Dora's inquiring gaze, an enchanting smile spread across her beautiful face.

"Hello, I'm Dora. Welcome to our open house. Do you have any questions I might answer?"

"Oh, hi—I'm Dottie Johns. I live in Leming, but I was visiting friends in Mondale, and heard about the Brooks open house. I used to live here many years ago. I think I was six or seven years old at the time, and I remember this mailbox. Didn't it used to be on the road near the highway close to the maple tree?"

Dottie turned the key dangling from the lock and opened the hinged door of the box, peering inside.

"Yes, it was there. We found it when we cleared out all the overgrowth. Are you a member of the Grant family? Maybe you're related to my husband. He inherited this house from his father. The original builders were his grandparents."

"No, my parents rented the house. I don't know anything about the landlord. I was a kid and didn't pay much attention. We lived here maybe for a year or two and then moved somewhere else. We never stayed anywhere very long. I have some very nice memories of the time I spent playing under the big tree, and this mailbox was a huge part of my imagination."

"This is wonderful. I'm so happy you decided to come tonight. My husband and I have renovated it, and this is our open house for our new Brooks Bed & Breakfast. Tell me everything you remember about the house while your family lived here. There's so much we don't know."

"Like I said, I was just a kid. I escaped to the big old tree where it was quiet and peaceful, and I could play by myself. The mailbox wasn't used for real mail, but when I found it, it had mail. I couldn't read well enough to know what it was, but I didn't open any of it. I just pretended it was from relatives wanting to know how we were doing. I used to wear the key around my neck and tucked it in my shirt. It was my safety net when things were hard in the house. I left that very key in a drawer in my room. Someone must have found it and figured out that it went to the mailbox. I even had a little bag of money I found on the highway, and I figured out it was Mexican money. I made up a story about going to Mexico and going shopping. Oh, and there was Sally."

"Was she a friend from around here?"

"Sort of. She was another find I salvaged from the highway.

She was a doll. I kept her in my hideout under the tree. When my parents decided we were moving, I wanted to stop at the tree and get her, but they were in a hurry and didn't have time for me to dawdle, they said."

Dora's face lit up. "Dottie, come with me."

Dora went to the basement stairwell, turned on the light, and descended the sixteen stairs. In the corner was a worktable covered with projects. Dora took some time looking at the labeled boxes on the shelves. She pulled out a box labeled "*Suzy Q.*" and set it on the workbench. She removed the lid, and carefully withdrew a doll. She was sure it must be Sally. She lovingly handed the doll to Dottie.

"Sally," the young woman exclaimed. "You found her, and she looks amazing. Oh, this is so much fun."

Dottie embraced her long-lost friend and then went to Dora and hugged her as well.

"We found the doll when we cleared out the shrub around the maple tree. That's when we found the mailbox, too. The key was in a trunk we rescued from the attic. The only thing I don't have is the pesos we found in a little money bag. I'm afraid I gave them away to a friend going to Mexico a long time ago."

"This is so amazing. I never thought I would see my doll again. Tonight, when I drove past the maple tree, I could see that everything was different and figured it was all in a landfill somewhere by now. I don't care about the pesos, but I'm happy to see Sally again."

Dottie handed the doll back to Dora.

"No, she's yours. Keep her. I called her Suzy Q. It's a pet name my husband used for me, a leftover from our teenage years. Sally fits her better. She's your doll, you take her home."

"Oh, Mrs. Grant, thank you. You've no idea what this means to me. This house has held some painful memories, but finding

Sally, seeing the little mailbox, meeting you, and taking in the aura of this house has melted my heart quite a bit."

Dora's phone beeped with a notification message.

"Excuse me while I see if this needs my attention."

"Sure, that's fine," Dottie nodded.

Dora read the message, reminding her of the meeting she had scheduled in the library.

"Dottie, could we get together for lunch soon? I'd love to hear more about you and your time at Brooks. Can I call you in a few days and set something up? I can come to Leming, so you don't have to make another trip here."

"I'd like that, Mrs. Grant, I'd like that very much. What is your phone number?"

The two exchanged phone numbers, hugged one more time, and with Sally cradled in Dottie's arms, they ascended the basement stairs.

Dottie got in line at the buffet table.

Dora walked to the library, wondering what her trio had up their sleeves. She noticed they had been unusually carefree of late. She had decided to let well enough alone and figured they were busy with party plans. She entered the library and saw the group closing ranks. Dora took the bull by the horns, so to speak, and asked, "What's going on?"

Jean handed Dora a large white envelope.

"Open it," she said. "See what's inside."

Dora opened the envelope's flap and removed three official-looking certificates from *Thorup Career Institute*. Each certificate proclaimed the named individual as having completed training in Private Investigation. The artistry of calligraphy spelled out each one, and there was an embossed gold seal on each certificate. Three pairs of eyes looked on, waiting for Dora's approval.

"Are you guys telling me that you've all become private investigators?

"Dora, I did a good job finding out about that Davis broad, right?"

"Yes, Jean. You did an excellent job."

"Well, I got to thinking, and I know I said I didn't want to work anymore, but I enjoyed the Davis assignment. I decided to get my license and be a PI. Dora, there aren't any PIs in Mondale. The market is wide open, and the city needs me. When I told Eva and Old Abe what I wanted to do, they decided to join me. Eva will be my Girl Friday, and Old Abe will help wherever needed."

"Look, it's great that you guys want to work together, and if you want to be PI's, it's okay by me. I ask that you not allow it to interfere with my bed-and-breakfast."

Jean quickly responded, "Don't worry, you won't even know we're here. We'll keep our cases at a manageable level, and we won't bother your guests." She held up her pointer finger, "And, in exchange for office space, we're prepared to be on call with our services at any hour. You can be our manager, so to speak."

"Office space, manager? Look, guys, I need the bedrooms in this house for guests, I can't spare a room for that. If you require office space, you'll need to find it elsewhere, and I don't have time for another job."

"Dora, we won't require anything of you. I just offered the manager title to sweeten the deal. We know you'll be busy, so we'll manage ourselves. Regarding the office space, I found space in the basement. It will be perfect, and it won't cost you a thing. The three of us are pooling our money, and we'll wall off a section."

Dora looked at Eva. "Mom, is this something you want to do?"

"At first, I was doubtful, but taking those classes online was fun, and I've decided I want to do it. Don't worry, Dora, I'll keep this ragtag group in line."

"Yeah, Mom, and who'll keep you in line?"

Old Abe immediately raised his hand and, with a glint in his one good eye, declared, "I'll volunteer for that job because I do some of my best work undercover," he said, winking at Eva.

Eva blushed and good-naturedly jabbed the older man in the ribs.

"If you don't mind, Abe, I don't want to hear about it," said Dora.

The three new detectives hugged each other, jumping up and down as though they were arthritic cheerleaders celebrating a winning high school football game.

"Look, I want you to play by the rules, so get a business license immediately. By the way, do you have a name for your business?"

The threesome locked arms and stomped in a power stance they had practiced. In unison, they declared, "We are Justice Finders."

"Justice Finders, huh? Heaven, help us." Dora shook her head. The trio of crime fighters maintained their pose.

"I'm going for a walk in the garden if you need me. I need to get some air and wind down a bit. Would the *Justice Finders* keep the party going without me for a while?"

Eva broke rank and hurried to her daughter. Jean waved as she headed toward the kitchen, and Old Abe trailed behind.

"You want some company?" asked Eva.

"No, Mom, I'd like to be myself. Today is a special anniversary for me and Len. I purposely planned this open house as a way of celebrating. I know he had something like this in mind for me himself. I'm going to one of the reflection benches and sit with my thoughts for a while. My life has changed so much in the last six months, and I see more changes coming. I'm barely starting to process it all. I love the garden. It's where I feel peace in a boisterous world."

Eva took hold of Dora's shoulders an arm's length away and forced direct eye contact. A gravity-laden tear found its way steadily down Dora's chin.

"Dora, you are the strongest person I know. I've seen you change before my very eyes from a dependent wife to an independent woman adjusting to her circumstances. I'm proud of you. You've handled yourself with dignity and poise. You go on out to Len's Garden and reflect. Pretend Len is there. Have a good talk, and cry if you need to. Go on, I'll keep your party lively."

Dora stepped through the doorway and made her way to the garden entry. She was surprised to find Abe there.

"Hey, Ms. Dora. It's a fine evening out here."

"Hi, Abe. What are you doing out here? You should be inside partying with the rest of them," said Dora.

"Oh, I've been partying, Ms. Dora. These days, it only takes a little for me to get partied out. I just came out to get a breath of air. I was on my way back inside. Gotta keep my women happy."

"You are a charmer, Abe. I'll bet you always have been. Seriously, I appreciate how good you are with my mom. I know she can be a handful, but you make her laugh, and I love you for that."

"Your mom is my special lady, Dora. I want you to know that. I like to joke around with all the women. It makes them feel special, but Eva is exceptional. And you, my young friend, are a chip off the old block."

"Save that charm for your harem. I'm going for a walk."

"I'd offer to accompany you, but I sense you want to be alone, so I'll return to the party. Have a good walk, milady."

Abe made a courtly bow, and Dora modestly lifted her skirts in a mocked curtsy, delicately stepping past the old gentleman and taking the path to the garden.

31

Love conquers fear, like the sun breaks
through the morning fog.

AMBIENT LIGHTING lined the pathway, and flower gardens danced courtesy of the power of the daytime sun and evening breezes. Hardwired garden lanterns marked the reflection benches. Dora felt a pull toward Len's favorite spot, the sensory station located the furthest out. As she found her way to it, she felt compelled to hum an old, familiar song she first heard many years ago. It was at a drive-in in the company of a sixteen-year-old boy who spent the night trying to make her laugh about the silliness of romance. Dora sat on the bench, closed her eyes, and brought the memory into view. She continued to hum and then stopped to voice her thoughts.

"I miss you, Len. I miss you so much."

She smiled with tender thoughts about a man gone too soon.

"I love you, Dora."

Those words did not come from her imagination. They were spoken in Len's voice. She opened her eyes, and there before her was the image of Len, though slightly fuzzy. It was Len, she had no doubts about it. She jumped up and reached out.

"It's no use, Dora, you can't touch me, but it's me. My soul has been assigned to Brooks, and I can appear to you here. We can talk, but we live in two different spheres. It's the best I can do for now. You are so beautiful. I wish I could take you in my arms and whisper those words in your ear."

"Len," she said breathlessly, "this is almost perfect. It's the anniversary of our engagement. I have an open house going on inside. Somehow, I knew this would be something you would approve of. I have so much to tell you."

"I've been inside with your guests. The twins have grown since I left. They look like Roger when he was that age. I didn't see Robyn or Hannah. I didn't expect to see Robyn, but I'd hoped Hannah would be here."

"She's busy and still thinks this venture is a little foolish, but so many things have changed, and she's not as vocal about it anymore. Her expertise in money management has come in handy. Honestly, it's okay. She has her life, and Brooks is mine. But Robyn and the kids are fine. I'm making good use of that program the kids installed on your computer."

"Does it still croak like a frog?"

Dora nodded, and they laughed. She was struck by how casual and normal everything seemed. She was having a conversation and laughing with her husband, who died six months ago.

"Don't you think this is a little outrageous?"

Len fidgeted and nodded.

"I know all about the bonds, Dora. I'm glad Karvelas got that all worked out for you. I'm sorry about the mess I left with the bills. Initially, I hoped to pay back everything with profit of our business venture. That's why I was so all-fired, determined to get it up and running. I needed to get the revenue coming in. Then, when I found out the value of the bonds, I breathed a little easier, knowing we had a windfall to get me out of hot water. But life, or I should say death, got in the way. I know things were hard for you, but I'm so proud of you, Dora. You kept your head and plowed through, figuring things out yourself. You are a formidable woman."

"Yeah, well, sometimes we do things we have to do. What I learned from all this is to not give in to pessimism, to persevere in the face of adversity, and to keep looking for a better answer."

Dora stopped, motioned with her arms at the garden, and gestured toward the house, where the windows lit up with party lights.

"Len, Brooks looks wonderful. I never properly recognized your work here. I know Roger helped a lot, but I see you in everything about this place. I love the reflection benches, and I found the plans you drew for the garden lighting. I hope I got it right."

"Everything looks perfect. I wouldn't change a thing."

"Len, I have so many questions. What's it like where you are? Are the streets paved with gold? Do you get to sit in the clouds, and have you learned to play a harp? What do you do all day? There are so many things I want to know." She stopped and, with reverence in her voice, asked, "Have you met Him?"

Dora had an honest look of questioning and waited for a response. Len slowly smiled and answered.

"It's wonderful, Dora. You'll see for yourself someday, but that's a long way off. For now, trust me that it will all be worth the wait."

Len stretched out his arms in her direction.

"The world needs you. You, my love, are just getting started in fulfilling your purpose."

He stopped and took a step closer.

"I see you're wearing the necklace."

Dora grasped the stone dangling from her neck and traced the letters with one finger.

"I found it in the box you brought down from the attic. I wish I knew its history. I saw the picture of your grandparents, and I think your grandmother wore this necklace in that picture. Beyond that, there's just something about it. I've not taken it off since I took it out of the box."

Len responded, "I wrote something for you. Would you like to hear it?"

"Yes, of course."

Dora had not taken her eyes off Len. As he spoke, she continued her gaze, absorbing his words as he looked back at her.

"It's titled **Best Girl** —

In the quiet of the meadow, under skies so blue,
There walks a girl whose beauty, shines like morning dew,
It softly settles on the earth, with a gentle grace,
And eyes that hold the secrets of a simple sacred place.

Her laughter, like the river, flows pure toward the sea,
As she dances neath the trees, she is so wild and free.
Her hair, a golden sunset, glistens in the evening light,
A radiant glow that guides me all throughout the night.

With hands that tend to gardens, nurturing every bloom,
She's the keeper of the forest, banishing all the gloom.
Her spirit, like the mountains, is solid, secure, and true,
She leads me through the valleys to skies of azure blue.

She's my Best Girl, a heart of gold, a soul so kind,
In her presence, I feel peace, and a joy that is divine.
In her eyes, I see the stars, they shine and brightly gleam,
And in her love, for me I've found my truest, fondest dream.

So, let's wander, hand in hand, through massive fields of green,
Where nature's melody, the sweetest song, always can be seen.
For in your arms, I truly have found my sacred place,
Dora, you're my Best Girl, my love, my saving grace."

Dora sat breathlessly, lingering at the artistry of the words spoken as though a blessing were being pronounced upon her brow.

"Len, it's exquisite, I love it. I hope you wrote it down somewhere."

"I did. It's on a piece of paper in the drawer by the bed. I meant to copy it into my journal but got distracted, you know, with death."

They both chuckled.

"I want to read it over and over," said Dora. "Len, come home with me? I don't want to be away from you ever again."

"I can't, Dora. I have to stay here. That may be an option as I progress in my orientation. But my influence will be wherever you need me. This worked out well for us. That's another box I can check off in this orientation thing. I love you. I always have, and I always will. We've made a pretty good team."

Len looked around as though checking to be sure they were alone. "I have to go, Dora, but I must tell you one more thing. I know the secret of aging."

"You what?"

"I know why some people age so fast and noticeably, and others seem to be the persona of youth. Remember when we were young and were always looking forward to something? We looked forward to being old enough to get a driver's license, finishing school, meeting someone special, getting that promotion, having kids, going on a special vacation, and then being able to retire. There was always something to look forward to. We age when we stop looking forward to the next big thing and become numb to our circumstances. Dora, there are so many things about eternal existence humanity can look forward to. That's why it's referred to as *eternal*, because there's always something to look forward to."

"Len, I want to be with you. Do something so I can be there, too."

"No, Dora. It's not your time. You still have a purpose here on earth. You are so good at helping people. You've always been able to sense what needs to be done. My work is on the other side of the veil. Remember that you have a lot to look forward to. I'm being called back, I need to go, but you'll see me again. I love you. Think Celestial, Dora, that's the key."

Dora wiggled her nose, their old secret form of communication. "I love you, too, Len."

He dissipated in front of her eyes and melded into the atmosphere. Music wafted through the air, and the evening breeze wrapped her with a cloak of balmy bliss. She touched the pebble on her neck and traced the etched initials, BG — Best Girl — Best Guy.

The End

A sneak peak into the second book
in the seasons of *Brooks* series

BROOKS
Bed & Breakfast

1

Seek not just success, but purpose. For true fulfillment lies not in the pursuit of wealth or fame, but in the pursuit of meaning —a calling that ignites the soul and lights the path ahead.

"Good morning, Iris. What's for breakfast today? It smells heavenly."

Good morning, Ms. Dora. I've got a frittata in the oven. It should be ready in another fifteen minutes. I'm serving it with avocado toast, sweet potato hash browns, and a fruit salad. And, of course, we have the usual oatmeal, toast, hard-boiled eggs, milk, coffee, and tea for those preferring something more traditional."

Dora nodded briefly. "I heard Roy singing in the garden this morning. Sounds like he's in his usual chipper mood."

"Oh yes, Ms. Dora. He loves that garden. He's getting it ready for winter weather."

"My Len used to sing gospel music when he worked outside. He thought that to be the closest place to being in Heaven while on Earth."

Dora's attention went to the corner of the kitchen, where she smiled at Len, her spirit-bodied husband, who looked on in rapt attention. She was the only one to see him, and they both knew that. It was their secret romance, and often, Dora was caught grinning like a schoolgirl, and she would make up stories to explain. She usually left her interrogators walking away shaking their heads at her feeble excuses.

She wiggled her nose in Len's direction, and he blew her a kiss that she had caught and tucked into her apron pocket.

"Ms. Dora, are you swatting flies? I don't allow flies in my kitchen. I hope Roy didn't leave that screen door ajar. I'll be all over that man like mayonnaise on a bologna sandwich."

"Oh no, Iris. It wasn't a fly. The sun blinded me for a second. I'll check the screen door for you. Is there anything I can do to help this morning?"

"No, Dottie and I have everything taken care of. She is making sure the serving table is spread proper. We have two couples today, and I expect they'll be coming down right away."

When Dora started seeking help for her new venture, this couple were among the first to apply. As part of their interview, Iris whipped up an impromptu meal using available pantry items while her husband, Roy, regaled Dora with his thoughts about groundskeeping. By the end of the interview, Dora knew she had found her cook and groundskeeper. She had built four casitas on the property and offered one for them to live in. In their mid-sixties and their family raised, they wanted to work for another ten years before considering retirement. To Dora, their positive attitude about Brooks was heaven-sent.

Tall, with a full beard and strawberry-blond hair both streaked with gray, Roy's body had been hardened with years of hard work. He was a well-educated engineer but preferred to work outside and get his hands in the dirt.

Loaded with energy and positivity, Iris had raised a passel of children as a stay-at-home mother. With her legendary cooking skills, she could whip up a hearty meal and loved using fresh ingredients from the garden.

Dottie Johns parents were squatters and had lived in the Brooks house when she was a child. Dora met her at the Brooks open house, and they instantly struck up a friendship. By all indications, Dottie had a difficult childhood, and she needed a job. Dora hired her and she had proven her worth over and over.

Dottie lived in one of the casitas as well. A sweet girl, she looked to Dora as a mother figure. Dora was all too happy to take on that role.

Dora's son Roger and his wife, Ann owned and operated a hardware store in Leming, a few hours north of Mondale. Dora's grandsons were their twin fourteen-year-old boys, Luke and Devon.

Hannah, Dora's second child, is single and lives in Chicago where she works for a major investment company.

Her youngest child, Robyn lives in Australia with her Air Force husband, Brian and three children under the age of eight. They have two girls Rachel and Liz and their little boy Lenny, named after his grandpa Len.

Dora's mother, Eva, a bundle of energy, lives in the Mondale Assisted Living Center, and sees her daughter often.

The Justice Finders, a private investigator team consisting of Dora's best friend Jean, and friends Eva and Abe. Their business had proved to be an interesting diversion.

"Good morning Ms. Dora," Dottie appeared to be her usual cheery self.

"Good morning, Dottie. It's a beautiful day, and you look very pretty today."

"Thank you, Ms. Dora. Is there anything you need me to do today aside from the usual?"

"No but check with Iris to see if she needs help. I know we're expecting a full house this coming weekend."

"Okay, I will."

"Do you have something planned for today?"

Dottie shrugged. "Well, sort of. I heard from an old—uhm—friend and thought I might get away this afternoon for a catch-up session."

"I hope it all works out; old friends are the best."

"Thanks, Ms. Dora."

The footsteps on the staircase diverted the Dora's attention to the dining area, and everyone hopped to action.

"Time to go to work," Iris boomed. "I have the frittata. Dottie, you grab that fruit salad. Ms. Dora, would you mind bringing in the avocado toast platter? I'll come back for the hash browns I left in the warming oven. Everything else is out and ready."

Dottie finished working and, by early afternoon, entered her casita to shower before heading out the door for her meeting with Eddie Jacobs. A few days ago, she was surprised to get a phone message from her old friend, Gwen Phillips, who had told her that Eddie was back in town and wanted to see Dottie. Initially, she said she wasn't interested, but Gwen convinced her that she needed to see him one last time and make sure he understood Dottie's boundaries.

She called the phone number Eddie left with Gwen, and now she was ready to have a final confrontation with him. She felt stronger than those days five years ago, and she was confident she was in a better place. She didn't need Eddie in her life now, nor could she see any reason to believe he belonged in her future.

She walked out the door and climbed into the car Ms. Dora had made available for her use. The *Brooks Bed & Breakfast* logo and contact information were emblazoned on the vehicle's doors, and Dottie was proud of her association with the business.

When she called Eddie yesterday, she told him to meet her at the Lark Nest Café in Mondale, a fifteen-minute drive for her. During the drive, she remembered events from five years ago, and an old, familiar hardness formed around her heart while tears rappelled down her cheeks.

Five years ago, she had prayed Eddie Jacobs would rot and hoped awful things would happen to him.

Dottie parked the car in front of the café and walked inside. She was immediately drawn to a booth at the end of the room occupied by a man she barely recognized and yet was sure of his identity.

Eddie had changed. He was no longer the skinny, pimply faced boy man she thought she couldn't live without those many years ago. He still had long, sandy-colored hair that cascaded down his shoulders and still danced with every movement as if caught in a perpetual breeze.

However, now he sported a beard as untamed as his hair. His shirt clung to his frame, accentuating the contours of a toned physique. He exuded the same effortless confidence that she knew all too well. His dreamy eyes, his most captivating feature, still had the appearance of pools of warmth holding untold secrets, and they still sparkled with a hint of mischief.

She felt like a robot staring into his smile; meant to melt even the coldest heart.

But Dottie's was frozen. She reminded herself that Eddie Jacobs was a dreamer, a wanderer, a free spirit guided by the whims of the universe. He rose from his seat, motioning for her to join him.

Dottie stopped for a few seconds to muster her courage and reconfirm her resolve, and then she slowly made her way towards Eddie. *How could he be so casual?*

Did he not remember what had happened? Dottie's grief surfaced briefly, and then she tucked it away, where it resided, covered by sheer willpower.

"Dottie, I'm glad to see ya girl. Ya look great. Come here and hug me."

Dottie quickly slid into the booth to escape his open arms. She ducked her head, not wanting to look into those eyes, and sat close to the edge so Eddie wouldn't assume he could sit next to her. His welcoming smile faded, and he returned to his seat on the opposite side of the booth.

"Thanks for coming. I just wanted to say hello and make sure you're okay. I went to our old place and Gwen told me you're doin' real good. She said ya have a great job. I'm glad. I've always wanted ya to be happy, ya know that. I still think about ya, Dottie, honest I do. I got out of prison a few months ago, and I wanted to look ya up right away but kept putting it off. Then I thought, Eddie, you need to say hi to Dottie."

He stopped talking and stared at her for a few seconds.

"Please look at me, baby. We had some good times before …"

"Eddie, I came here for one reason."

Dottie slowly brought her eyes level with his and was relieved there was nothing in that gaze like she was afraid there might be. Her heart didn't soar, her brain didn't freeze, there were no goosebumps, and her tongue wasn't tied. She felt free—completely free from his hold. She always assumed she would revert to the muddle-headed schoolgirl who had messed up her life with childish emotions. Instead, she felt like a woman in charge of her destiny. She put herself first and wouldn't allow anyone to control her.

"Eddie, you're a part of my past, and I've left that behind. What happened between us is ancient history. You are part of the most painful thing I've ever been through. I suppose I could have told you all this over the phone, but I honestly wanted to look you in the eyes and know for myself that it's over for me, and it is Eddie; it's over. That's all I wanted to say. Now, excuse me, I'm going back to my life. Good luck, Eddie."

Dottie grabbed her shoulder bag and stood.

"Dottie, wait. Let's just talk for a while. I've missed ya, baby. I just want to talk."

"There's nothing to say, Eddie. Please let me be."

She proceeded to the front door of the café. The waitress was wiping down the counter when Dottie walked past.

"Hi, Dottie. Good to see you. Give Dora my best."

"Good evening, Lark – I'll do that."

Dottie smiled, waved to the woman, and then walked out the door and to her car. She breathed deeply and smiled with an added level of confidence.

Eddie watched as Dottie pulled away in the car labeled *Brooks Bed & Breakfast, 239 Grouse Road, call 555-883-4587.* He grabbed a crayon from the holder at the table and hurriedly scribbled the information on the unused napkin. His attention was diverted to the waitress approaching his booth.

"Do you want more coffee, or are you ready to order some food?"

"I'll have more coffee and a bill. I won't be staying for dinner."

Eddie spent another half hour sipping his coffee and thinking about Dottie and what she had said.

Man, things have sure changed.

Acknowledgments

I am very grateful for the invaluable expertise of everyone at Author Ready Services. From the weekly writer's group sessions to monthly mentoring sessions with Mr. Richard Paul Evans, I've met people who have a zest for creativity in the literary world. I've been so impressed with their willingness to help me achieve my goal.

Debbie Ihler Rasmussen as my editor. She has been quick to answer questions and steer me steadily forward in my journey to be a published author.

Kim Autrey for making sure my punctuation, spelling and grammar were up to speed.

Francine Platt for making my book interior sparkle.

The services of 99designs and particularly Beyond Imagination for the beautiful cover created to showcase Brooks.

Brad Neufeld for helping me figure out how to showcase Brooks to the public.

Author Bio
and Expanded Dedication

I have always been a writer. I've written short stories, poems, essays, and family histories, but I did them all in between the juggling of family responsibilities. Finding myself in an empty nest is where I gave birth to a budding passion for literary creativity. I awake every morning wanting to write. My nocturnal dreams are of visionary tales. That is how Brooks was conceived, born, nurtured, and came to be. This is my first work of fiction, but it will not be my last. I've started to bring a sibling to life for the house called Brooks.

I struggled to come up with a proper dedication page. Not that I couldn't think of anyone to thank, but that there are so many people I need to express gratitude towards. My husband is always an obvious first choice because he encourages me to follow my heart in things I want to do. He is my biggest cheerleader and scolds me when I get down on myself. According to him, I am formidable, and in my continuing quest to figure out what he means by that, I've been blessed with his unfailing support. We enjoy the warmth of retired life in southern Utah, with frequent visits from our children and grandchildren.

Beyond that, I decided to name most of the characters in this book with family names as a way of dedication. However, I have more family members than characters. Therefore, my next book will feature the names of those who didn't make the cut this time.

Plus, I dedicate this book to my daughter, Robyn, and my daughter-in-law, Roseann. The former lost her battle with cancer five years ago, and the latter died in a horrific accident a year ago. Both are likely chanting "Mom" in another realm of our eternal journey as they applaud the publication of my first work of fiction.